OA

Consent Of The Governed

Book Three

B. D. Lutz

© 2022 B.D. Lutz.

ISBN: 978-1-7352793-5-0

This is a work of fiction. Names, characters, businesses, places, events, locales, and incidents are either the products of the author's imagination or used in a fictitious manner. Any resemblance to actual persons, living or dead, or actual events is purely coincidental. All rights reserved. No part of this publication may be reproduced, distributed, or transmitted in any form or by any means, including photocopying, recording, or other electronic or mechanical methods, without the prior written permission of the publisher, except in the case of brief quotations embodied in critical reviews and certain other non-commercial uses permitted by copyright law.

All rights reserved. Except as permitted under the U.S. Copyright Act of 1976, no part of this book may be reproduced, scanned, transmitted, or distributed in any form or by any means, or stored in a database or retrieval system, without the prior written permission of the publisher. Please do not participate in or encourage piracy of copyrighted materials in violation of the author's rights.

Contact the author via email: CLELUTZ11@gmail.com

ACKNOWLEDGEMENTS

I'd like to thank my friends, family, and you for your support. A special thanks to Heidi, Darline, Sharon, Steve, Russ, Aundre, Tim, Charley, and Sean. Without your encouragement, this simply doesn't happen.

To the American Military: Without you standing watch over this great nation, this book may not have been possible. You do what few among us have the courage to do. Thank you.

Edited by Monique Happy Editorial Services
www.moniquehappyeditorial.com

Thank you for your hard work and guidance.

Cover designed by: Kelly A. Martin
www.kam.design

Kelly, you are a master at your craft!

Image Credits:
PantherMediaSeller (DepositPhotos), Aliven (DepositPhotos), Lesterman (Shutterstock)

Prologue

Eight Months Post Inauguration, Camp Lejeune

First Sergeant Killian Callahan clutched the folded paper tightly. His complexion now matched his deep red high-and-tight. His twenty-four-year military career had just ended by force. Being a Marine was all he knew. Following in his father's footsteps, Killian enlisted the day he turned eighteen. Today, he exited MARSOC Headquarters as a civilian.

Opting to walk, he left his car behind and stormed onto Command Drive. He hoped the eleven-mile walk to his home on Texas Court would bleed off his urge to break something and bring his raging emotions under control.

Taking a hard right onto Horn Road, his pace quickened towards Marines Road. Once he crossed over Tank Trail onto Marines Road, his stride quickened to a jog. As the Marine Corps Engineering School materialized to his left, he broke into a full run.

The package, wrapped in plain brown paper and given to him by his Commanding Officer after signing Killian's Form 85SHD-Semi-Honorable Discharge papers, slapped against his thigh in rhythm with his pumping legs.

He recounted the conversation, but his confusion surrounding it didn't clear. *You've been hand-selected to receive a parting gift. Do NOT allow it to be seen. Do NOT open it until you exit Camp Lejeune. You'll find directions inside the package. Play the game for now, First Sergeant.*

He became aware of the paper still clutched in his right hand. His CO told him it related to the package and the two must remain separate at all times. He shoved the paper into his shirt pocket and picked up his pace.

Sweat drenched his Marine Corps Battle Dress Uniform as he pushed his body forward. He broke left onto Sneads Ferry Road and realized his plan wasn't working; his anger was building. His mind drifted back to the first time he'd seen combat during Operation Phantom Fury, the second battle of Fallujah, as part of Regimental Combat Team One. He'd taken shrapnel in his upper thigh in the same blast that claimed the life of his best friend. He watched many more Marines from RCT 1 make the ultimate sacrifice during those twelve days of hell. They died for their flag. A flag that was now viewed as a symbol of oppression and hate.

His initial deployment to the Iraqi theater set the tone for a career of honor and political sidestepping. He recognized early in his service that soldiers were puppets and the suits in DC pulled their strings. People possessing neither the courage nor intelligence to serve in the wars they created while standing on the plush carpeting of the Capitol Building controlled his life.

Killian considered leaving the Corps when his first enlistment ended but found a glimmer of hope in a brash Lieutenant Colonel who would later reach Full Bird. Their meeting was happenstance but forever changed his attitude toward his purpose as a Marine.

"Son, Marines are the line in the sand. No matter the reason our politicians set us loose, we represent hope for the hopeless."

As he crossed the point where Sneads Ferry transitioned to Wilson Boulevard, he fumed at his CO's words. *"According to Eden, your political affiliation is undesirable. The administration is moving towards a politically neutral military led by fair and politically neutral officers."*

He'd put the lives of the men and women under his command on the line countless times to preserve the freedoms he could no longer enjoy. The very freedoms now used to end his career.

He hit the pedestrian path on the bridge spanning Wallace Creek an hour and twenty minutes into his run. If his legs didn't give out, he'd be home in ten minutes. His focus shifted to finishing his run before fatigue won out, freeing his thoughts from the devastating news he'd received.

He rounded the corner from Bicentennial Avenue to Texas Court and slid to a stop. An 85 Movers truck sat in his home's driveway. Two men wearing gray jump suits rested on the box truck's front passenger side fender.

Adrenalin surged through his body as reality hit him. They were here to move him off base. Rubbery legs carried him towards the men. He had already determined which of the two he'd neutralize first.

"You better have a damn good reason for being parked in my driveway," Killian started, forcing his voice to remain calm. "Because I don't recall hiring movers."

A runt of a man pushed off the fender and said, "Killian Callahan, we're here to move your belongings to your new dwelling." A greasy smile broke across his face. "So pack your shit and move, double-time. We've been waiting on your ass long enough."

Sweat dripped down Killian's face as he continued his march in the runt's direction. He wasn't Killian's primary target a moment ago, but he'd just adapted his plan. "Check your attitude, Tiny."

The second mover, the larger of the two and Killian's initial target, burst into laughter. "Yeah, Tiny, check that bad little attitude of yours." After his amusement passed, he took a more serious tone. "Mister Callahan, we apologize for the confusion. Your CO should have told you what was happening."

"Look," Killian interrupted. "My career just ended an hour ago. This is my home. I expected to be shown some common courtesy and allowed to find someplace else to live."

"The BHR has assigned you a new resident dwelling," Tiny barked. "You're moving to gov-issued housing: Block One, Section Seven. Now, start packing. We have three more stops on this shit-hole base today." His smile returned before he continued. "Please pack your valuables real good. Wouldn't want anything happening to them during your move."

"You're moving me to government housing projects? You must be out of your minds."

Killian set a challenging stare on Tiny when movement to his right pulled his attention to the second gray-suited man. He locked eyes with Killian, gave a slight shake of his head, and mouthed, "Play the game."

Chapter 1

January 3rd, Twenty-Three Months Post Inauguration
NoDa Neighborhood, Charlotte

Callahan read the text on his satellite phone and nodded. "Weapons hot." The sound of rounds being chambered and suppressors threaded was his team's response; they were ready.

"Remember your training. We neutralize everyone in the house. We've got zero intel on total combatants, so all eyes." Killian waited as the three members of their four-man squad confirmed their understanding.

From the driver's seat, he glanced to his right. "MM, you're with me. Phelps, you and Sylvan cover the rear exit. You'll enter on my command. Eliminate anyone who tries to escape."

"Why do you keep calling me MM, Callahan? Seriously, it's been, what, a year and a half? I thought Marines were supposed to be tough, but you're acting like a … crossing guard at an all-girls school. A girls school that hires girls as crossing guards. Thin-skinned crossing guards, to be exact."

MM, whose actual name was Steven Phillips, had earned the nickname MM because he was one of the Bureau of Harm Reduction moving men who'd relocated Callahan from his home on Camp Lejeune to a family cabin in Cornelius, North Carolina.

Callahan nearly ended up in government housing, but Phillips had pulled him aside and asked him to think long and hard about any place other than the gov-housing units. It wasn't until he looked around his house that he remembered the cabin. A picture of his dad holding his prized Striped Bass pulled from Lake Norman set his future in motion.

He had Phillips and Tiny reroute him to the place he now called home. Tiny, a gung-ho BHR loyalist, objected to the long-haul and nearly derailed his plan. From his front yard, Callahan called his former CO and, within minutes, a Form 85DRR- Dwelling Relocation Request was filed and approved. He found out later that Phillips helped push it through the BHR system, bypassing the Bureau of Equitable Housing review and locking down the approval in under an hour.

But he never let Phillips forget who his employer was. The man was invaluable to their plan, but it was simply too much fun busting his balls. The only other person aware of Phillips' double life had just sent him the text that would change everything.

"And that, MM, is why they hired me. Someone has to keep you girls safe. After all, your Army training is, well, Army training," he quipped as he pulled the latch and pushed his door open.

The instant his feet hit the pavement on East 37th Street in Charlotte's NoDa neighborhood, Callahan morphed into a Marine. His team went silent, moving as he'd ordered.

"Remember, this is only the beginning. We don't win this war tonight, we start it," he whispered over their coms as he approached their target's front door.

"Open up! This is the Citizen Soldier Patrol for Sector F9," Callahan yelled after three open-handed slaps on a flimsy screen door. After a quick ten-count, he slammed his palm against the door again. "We must speak to CS Squad Leader Fink immediately. It's urgent; we will enter by force if necessary."

His statement and pounding were responded to by a light flaring to life on the second floor, followed by heavy footfalls approaching the door. Callahan stepped back and pulled his suppressed weapon, holding it to his side.

"What the hell are you doing? Are you crazy waking me up at this hour?"

"I apologize for the intrusion. Are you SL Fink?"

"I am! What do you wa—"

A 9mm round crushing his frontal lobe cut Fink's question short.

"Primary down. Moving to secondary targets," Callahan whispered into his helmet's boom-mic. "Eyes on the rear egress."

A woman's voice reached Callahan as he dragged Fink's body into the cramped living room and shut the door. "Finn, is everything okay?"

"Finn Fink?" Phillips mouthed.

Callahan shrugged at Phillips' question, then pivoted towards the staircase. Creaking treads signaled their second target was coming to investigate. Callahan moved to the side of the enclosed staircase with his weapon drawn.

She didn't see her executioner. Her robed body crumpled to the hardwood floor the instant she reached the landing.

***

"His name was Alan. Finn must have been a nickname," Phillips said, holding the man's essential person pass up for inspection.

Confused, Callahan looked at his friend reclining in the passenger seat as he pulled the BHR sedan to a stop. "She called him Finn, right?"

"Gentlemen, same as before," Callahan said, ignoring Phillips' observation. "We have one more stop after this. Then we go home."

Chapter 2

2 a.m., January 3rd, West 14th Street Market

Emmitt Milo sat quietly in the cab of his aging twenty-four-foot box truck backed into the West 14th Street Market's loading docks. If the text telling him to move forward didn't come soon, he'd be forced to unload the truck and replace the supplies he'd spent the last two hours pilfering from the store—*his* store, the one he'd built into a thriving marketplace catering to the gentrification crowd.

Now under government control, it had become a lifeless generic food distribution center charging egregious amounts of money for necessities. His BHR observer, or *managing partner's*, explanation of the price increases had chilled Emmitt: *The government is supplying the natives with easy access to things we feel they should consume. For that, we must charge a premium. Most importantly, the civilians entering our establishment are suckling the government's teat and needn't worry their pearls over cost or selection.*

Shortly after being nationalized—a truth the observer avoided and called a partnership instead—the market began receiving what appeared to be government-produced foodstuffs clad in simple brown wrappers with black or blue lettering, reminiscent of the '80s government cheese program and screaming of pitiable quality.

Emmitt's catalyst for contacting his longtime friend, Willis Stinger, was his accidental discovery of a supplier invoice tucked haphazardly into the shrink-wrap of their third shipment that revealed Chinese Communist Party-owned Dai Chan Grocery Supply was now his store's main supplier.

Dai Chan had been snapping up American food producers for decades, a reality unknown to the average American. Emmitt wasn't your average American. He avoided doing business with them at all costs. Their products were inferior and often arrived spoiled, prompting him to move to locally sourced. He was the first in the Cleveland area to do so and he quickly defined what locally sourced truly encompassed. It wasn't a buzzword for Emmitt. He maintained stringent guidelines for what "local" meant. If a potential supplier was owned by a conglomerate but grew locally, they didn't get his business. If they so much as had investors from large companies, they didn't put their products on his shelves.

He was proud of what he'd built and what he brought to his community. That pride was the reason why what he'd be doing the instant he received the text would be bittersweet.

He stared at the building through the box truck's side-view mirror, remembering the day he signed the lease. He was twenty-two with his discharge papers tucked in the breast pocket of his Marine Corps Dress Blues. His service in Nam taught him a valuable lesson: if you want to do it, you do it now. Tomorrow could find you bleeding out on foreign soil. He remembered his grand opening, the friends he'd made, and the community he served. His memories ignited a fire in his belly.

"I built it. I'll end it," he whispered.

Concern seeped in; his friend should have texted by now. He tossed the matches to the bench seat and ran a hand down his face. Worry and frustration battling for control. Glancing at the dash-mounted clock, he decided he'd waited long enough. It was time to unload the hundreds of pounds of food tightly packed in the truck's cargo area.

He took hold of the door handle the very second his satellite phone flashed to life, displaying a single word: *Bonfire*.

Emmitt shifted the truck into first gear with a cringe-inducing grinding. "So much for stealth," he muttered as the truck lurched forward.

He engaged the truck's emergency brake at the parking lot's exit onto West 14th Street and jumped from the cab, matchbook in hand.

Eyes stinging, Milo set the entire matchbook ablaze and tossed it into the puddle of rubbing alcohol twenty feet from the building. He darted back to the truck cab as blue flame raced towards the market's shattered glass entrance.

As the truck bounced from the parking lot, Milo glanced into the side-view mirror to find his life's work already engulfed, the reddish-orange flames licking the night sky and serving as a crackling battle cry.

Chapter 3

2:30 a.m., January 3rd, Willis Stinger's Home

Lisa watched Willis. He was seated in the corner of the command center, his satellite phone bathing his face in its harsh light. He'd been typing furiously for fifteen minutes, making it impossible for her to sleep.

"I'll wrap up in a minute," he said, addressing her dagger-like stare.

"I'm more interested in what you're typing than sleeping," she answered.

UW responded with a smile, never taking his eyes off the phone.

"If you don't tell me, you'll need to leave. Or maybe I'll go on strike. The pay at this joint is pretty crappy and my boss—well, he's a jerk," she quipped.

"He is?" UW replied absently. "I hear the Bureau of Harm Reduction is hiring. Citizen Soldiers, too. Plenty of government work for a bright lady like yourself."

"Damn it, UW. Tell me what the hell's going on!"

"Check the exterior security cameras, the ones at the front of the house. Pan southwest."

Lisa sprang from her folding bed, taking a position in front of the monitors on her workstation. With a few keystrokes, the video feed switched from the front yard to an extended view across Lincoln Park. "Looks empty. What should I be seeing?"

As if on cue, a large box truck rumbled into view as it exited the West 14th Street Market's parking lot.

"Eyes on the building."

Lisa started at UW's voice over her shoulder. "Damn it, UW. Stop doing that!"

Her admonishment ended abruptly as a reddish-orange glow flared between the leafless trees skirting the Market's lot.

"What the hell!?" she shouted. "Someone set Emmitt's store on fire. We gotta call someone, the CS, anyone!"

"Somebody will call. It just won't be us."

Lisa swiveled her chair to face UW. "What's going on? You have to start letting us—or at least me—in on some of your plans. I'm stuck in this basement; the chances of me getting arrested and blowing the whole thing up are nil."

"I did. I told all of you we'd be mobbing them," UW answered through a wry smile.

Lisa's glare was meant to crack UW's granite veneer but merely elicited a soft chuckle.

"That may work on Jack, but he's soft—easily intimidated by strong women, however you want to say it. Me, on the other hand, I made grown-ass men cry for a living and I enjoyed it. So, park your peepers on the monitor."

Lisa, realizing she'd lost, turned back to the monitor in time to witness a massive explosion. Large sections of the market were launched in every direction as the sky burned bright with flame.

"Emmitt's safe," UW offered, responding to Lisa's shocked gasp. "He's dropping the food at his warehouse on Scranton. The place looks abandoned, but it isn't. Tomorrow, he plays the role of a distraught citizen until the BHR assigns him to a new store. Then, it starts over."

Lisa chewed her bottom lip, worry creasing her brow. "UW, we're bringing a lot of attention to our neighborhood. I'm not one to question your tactics, but is that wise?"

Meeting Lisa's worried gaze, Willis understood it was time to explain the full scope of his quickly unfolding strategy. Lisa was a ghost, a missing person, and he planned to keep it that way.

"What happened at Emmitt's—what we executed yesterday—is repeating across the country as we speak. Our excursion to the IX should have prompted the BHR to consolidate their forces to guard against another attack while they work to repair the substation. We shouldn't see them for a few days, possibly a week. We hit the CS hard as well. Our actions had no discernible pattern. According to my contacts, this should send their command and control into complete chaos. They're blind with no idea where to focus their reaction."

Awash in understanding, she grinned. "Mobbing."

Willis nodded. "The only unknown is the scale of their retaliation. I'd guess it should land somewhere between Mao and Stalin in brutality. It'll be difficult to watch, and they *will* ensure we watch. I expect mass arrests, public beatings, and even executions. It'll be the first real test of our resolve. They will target us. The government's need for Jack to manage Stinger Machinery won't last forever. Meaning we hit them again before they regroup. So, get that list Billy secured ready, the one with all the Citizen Soldier addresses."

The command center's door slid open, interrupting their conversation. Jack stood in the opening, blurry-eyed and sleep-disheveled. Answering their suppressed expressions, he held up his screeching gov-issued cell.

"Eden's dead."

Chapter 4

3 a.m., January 3rd, Raven Rock Military Complex

"Remember, Genus: After your intro, you'll become overwhelmed with emotion, unable to speak, and turn the proceeding over to me and Representative Cummings. You'll remain on camera, dabbing your mascara, but keep your mouth shut. Not a fucking peep. Understand?" Woods had been circling Genus nonstop for ten minutes, barking threat-laced instructions.

Genus' medication was administered the instant Woods started her rant. Its warmth engulfed her like a flannel blanket, sending the awful woman's voice to the background of her endorphin-addled brain. "Got it. Cry, act sad, let you take it from there," she whispered.

Her anxiety melted as she succumbed to her reality. She was an empty suit, a familiar talking head employed to calm the American people, and she'd be dead the moment her purpose was served. She'd meet the same fate as Eden, his entire family, and every member of his administration. They would use her death as proof that domestic terrorists continued running amok, threatening the safety of every American. She smirked at the thought most prevalent in her mind. *I hope they don't kill me the same way as Eden.* The indignity of swinging naked from a flagpole would prove too great to bear. She preferred a bullet to the back of her head. Of course, she'd dress for the occasion. Maybe her Chanel evening gown or possibly the Dolce cocktail dress with her Prada Cleo. Yes, the Dolce-Prada pairing would suffice.

"I'm going out in style," she mumbled. "You can count on it."

"Excuse me, *President* Genus. What did you say?" Cummings asked.

"Unimportant," Genus answered while waving off Cummings' query. "Let's get started. Where's my teleprompter?"

Woods ran a hand down her face, her patience for Genus' incompetence vanishing. "You said you understood! However, your question implies otherwise. Now listen to me carefully: You're introduced, you cry, we take over. If you can't wrap your head around that, maybe we no longer require your services."

"You're probably right, but I'm not dressed appropriately for my execution. So, I'll simply cry when we go live. Is that adequate?" Genus said as her foggy mind cleared.

Woods nodded sharply. "Yes, that's adequate. You're live in thirty seconds. Work on those tears."

***

Genus' mournful wailing overwhelmed Cummings' voice, cutting off her remarks to the nation. Cognizant they were currently live-streaming to every cell phone in America, as well as broadcasting on televisions around the globe, Cummings placed a reassuring hand on Genus' shoulder.

Behind her grief-stricken facade, she leaned close to Genus and whispered, "Do you require Alois to *escort* you to your quarters?"

Genus registered her words and their meaning as Cummings began squeezing her shoulder. The woman's comforting touch turned threatening and vice-like as she hissed in her ear.

To the viewer, Genus' response appeared heartfelt, possibly thankful. She placed her hand on Cummings' and raised her eyes to meet the woman's gaze. The moment, a tender exchange of shared grief. Genus' nails went unnoticed as they dug deep into Cummings' skin, forcing the woman to release her talons from the President's shoulder.

Marshaling her emotions, Genus faced the camera. "I beg your forgiveness," she said, voice strained as she addressed the American people. "You must think me a blubbering fool, but I ask you to see an emotionally raw person grieving the loss of a dear friend. Do not confuse my sorrow as weakness." She paused, dabbing a tissue to her mascara-splashed eyes. "Let us move forward. Representative Cummings, please continue."

Cummings, seated to Genus' right, glanced at Woods and exchanged a look of surprise with her counterpart.

"Thank you, President Genus. I'm sure the American people understand and share in your grief." She turned to face the camera, her features softening. "Thank you for joining us at this early hour. As you are aware, yesterday we lost our intrepid leader. Although he'd fallen ill several months ago, his illness played no part in his untimely passing. What I'm about to tell you is shocking. Many of you may find my words difficult to accept. However, I must speak the truth. Our dear President Eden was assassinated."

Cummings' effectual pause ended as Woods fidgeted impatiently.

"More frightening was our discovery of the involvement of his once trusted Chief of Staff, Thad Roberts. This heinous man conspired with the domestic terrorists we've worked valiantly to bring to justice. Make no mistake; these are the same terrorists responsible for plunging our beautiful country into these dark and troublesome times. Operating as a lone wolf cell, he infiltrated our government's highest levels. Roberts manipulated our intelligence data, covered his cohort's tracks, and rendered us blind in our battle for your safety. Rest assured, America, our retribution was swift and righteous. Chief of Staff Roberts was tried, convicted, and executed this morning. We took these extraordinary measures to spare your emotional condition and deliver a message to those with whom he connived. Our rapid response should serve as a warning to the repugnant among us: You will pay dearly for your actions."

Cummings' posture stiffened, her features growing dark. "You'll be hearing from Representative Woods momentarily. Her presentation contains graphic imagery. We ask that you prohibit young children and individuals easily upset from viewing these gut-wrenching images. I ask you to rest easy knowing your government is working every moment of every day to keep you safe. Representative Woods, please proceed."

Woods leaned close to Genus and spoke just loud enough for the viewers to hear. "President Genus, we understand if you'd rather retire to your quarters during my presentation."

Genus, caught off guard, stammered quietly, "I thought I was supposed—"

"You're a brave woman. A beautiful example of courage," Woods interrupted while gripping Genus' hand tightly. "Parents everywhere should raise their children in your likeness."

Tilting her head in adoration, Woods patted the President's hand and turned to face the camera. "As Representative Cummings warned, the imagery I'm going to share will be difficult to view. However, we feel strongly that you, the American people, should see firsthand the level of brutality our enemy is capable of."

With a stiff nod from Woods, the screen flashed to an image of a flagpole. Difficult to discern at first glance, the image became clear as they gave the viewer time to receive it. The shriveled, unclothed corpses of President Eden and the First Lady hung by their necks thirty feet above a small patch of grass. Below them flew a never-before-seen flag: an eagle clutching a single five-pointed star.

Genus' sharp gasp followed by her bellowing sobs preceded the image disappearing from view. It was replaced by Representative Woods' unsmiling visage.

"Be confident, America. Your government will not rest until all of the perpetrators of this heinous act face justice. You will notice in the coming days an increased presence of your government in all its capacities in our streets and neighborhoods. Our singular focus remains to return normality to our country." Glancing at Representative Cummings, she nodded. "Our purpose today is to pledge that your government is functioning, stronger than ever, and has wrapped her arms around you to guide you through these troublesome times."

Woods sat back in her chair, signaling Cummings to finish their joint address.

"Well said, Representative Woods. I'm honored to work at your side." Cummings turned to the camera as she finished praising Woods. "Over the coming days and weeks, we will do our very best to keep you apprised of our progress. At present, we have no plans to curtail our country's reopening. We must restore normalcy to those who have pledged their loyalty to our government and reward your allegiance. We implore you to convince your friends and family to join us in creating a One America."

Cummings paused and glanced at the women seated at her side. She smiled broadly while wiping her tearless eyes. "President Eden's legacy will live on. We will carry the torch of his righteous agenda. Your new president—your first woman president, President Genus—will guide us through these troublesome times. Although viewing was mandatory, we thank you, America, for joining us at this early hour."

As the national address ended, Woods turned to Genus. Gone was her empathy for the terrified woman still sobbing hysterically.

"Well done, though I suspect your emotion is fear for your life more than sadness over Eden's passing. Either way, it was very convincing. Going forward, we will record your public addresses in advance." Woods reached into her leather briefcase and retrieved a single piece of paper. "This is the script for your next public address, scheduled to be released on the twentieth. The video crew will arrive at Raven Rock tomorrow to begin recording. Prepare to project strength and instill confidence."

Hands trembling, Genus accepted the paper. Her mouth moved in silent speech as she read the words. The President's eyes went wide as her breath hitched, causing Woods to smile.

"I see you understand," Woods said. "You'll embrace it—eventually."

Chapter 5

3:45 a.m., January 3rd, Willis Stinger's Home

Jack set his gov-issued phone on the coffee table in Willis' basement. He, Lisa, and Willis huddled around it as they watched the early morning national address in absolute silence.

"Didn't see that coming. You?" Jack asked as the command center door clicked shut behind them.

"Honestly, no," Willis answered without making eye contact. "The only thing it changes is our timeline. We accelerate it. Lisa, we'll need to get the CS home addresses divided into two sets. I'll let you know who receives each set later this morning. I'll handle the distribution."

Jack glared at Willis disbelievingly. "You're kidding, right? If they launch an offensive, we don't stand a chance. They'll pick us off one by one in a matter of days."

Willis, unmoved by Jack's proclamation, gave a crooked grin. "Jack, they haven't a clue who they're searching for. What we watched was a threat designed to elicit the exact reaction you're having. They're on their heels and they'll lash out like angry children. They'll eventually come for us whether or not they believe we're terrorists. It's been their plan from the beginning and refusing to sign the 85LP guaranteed it'll happen. But they'll be unfocused. If we hit them again and again, their troops *will* start second-guessing orders, breaking ranks, and hiding in their basements. We strike now! Send a message that we're simply not intimidated. Show them they can't stop us."

Jack searched Willis' eyes, hoping to find any indication he wasn't serious. He found only an ice-cold stare. "Look, UW, I don't pretend to speak for all of us, but I'm still wrapping my brain around what happened. I killed someone! More men probably died in the explosion. I was hoping to use the next couple of days to decompress and clear my head."

UW cocked his head. His expression unreadable. "Jack, you didn't kill a person. You killed the enemy. An enemy suffering no qualms with taking your life or those of your family. You *cannot* view it any other way. We didn't start this war, Jack, but I sure as hell plan on winning it."

UW didn't wait for Jack's response and turned to leave.

"Lisa," he said over his shoulder as he waited for the security door to slide open. "Organize the list by address. I'll bring Randy up to speed at work later today and I'll text Billy."

***

Jack, perched on the edge of Lisa's bed, wondered again how she managed to get any sleep on the folding nightmare. "Are you okay with all of this?"

Lisa, seated at her workstation and typing furiously, didn't take her eyes off the laptop as she replied. "I have no issues at all, Jack. My conscience is crystal clear. They brought this on themselves."

"Lisa," Jack interrupted. "I shot a man in the head. A stroke of my trigger ended his life. How do I square that?"

Lisa turned to face her husband. "You think about everything they've taken from us, the families they've torn apart, and the lives they've ruined." She paused, her features turning hard. "Worked for me."

She held his gaze, waiting for her message to be received. When she saw understanding wash over him, she turned back to her laptop.

"Clean your gun, Jack."

Chapter 6

7 a.m., January 3rd, Stinger Machinery

Jack's body had declared war on his mind. Exhaustion and anxiety had dug trench lines, launching endless volleys in an unwinnable battle. The urge to lash out at any human within arm's length was quickly becoming impossible to control. How were they going to execute UW's plan with the government swarming the streets? What retaliation would Crestwater exact on them for being part of the terrorist ilk?

He stood, intent on escaping his office. He needed to bleed off the rage slowly building in his chest before the rest of the Stinger team arrived. A nice long walk in the frigid January air was in order.

As he entered the reception area and made for the exit, the door swung open and he nearly collided with Agent Crestwater.

"Don't speak, don't breathe, don't even look at me," Jack growled as he forced his way past a startled Crestwater.

"My word, Mister Stinger. None of us enjoy Mondays—especially after the tragic news—but that's hardly a reason to threaten your manager."

"Crestwater, you literally did all three of the things I ordered you not to do," Jack said as he slammed to a stop. "You're pressing your luck. Fair warning."

Jack locked onto Crestwater's eyes, delivering a silent challenge for the man to continue. He watched as the agent tried to hold his gaze and failed, his lower lip quivering in fear.

"Look," Jack said while shaking his head. "I'm just really upset by Eden's assassination. I feel gutted. When will this violence end?"

Crestwater placed a reassuring hand on Jack's shoulder. "I understand. I'm sorry I didn't recognize your distress. The news of Eden's death has shaken me to my core. I find solace in knowing that we're in President Genus' most capable hands and those of her extraordinarily talented Regional Representatives. Try focusing on that, Jack. It may help ease your suffering."

Jack fought the urge to retch at Crestwater's touch. Swallowing his throat-stinging bile, he said, "Why didn't our government declare a national day of mourning? Allow us time to reflect on our loss? To decompress?"

"I agree. We could have used a day away to reset our lives. But, I'm told that our representatives are going to announce a period of national mourning. Just hold on a couple more days, Jack. Help for your emotional state is forthcoming."

Jack gave a nod, the bizarre exchange calming his mind as his ruse solidified Crestwater's trust in him. "Thank you. I believe your kind words have tamped the embers of rage Eden's death had stoked."

***

At midday, Crestwater suddenly appeared in Jack's office wearing a pensive expression. "Jack, I have two items of importance to address. I hope you've recovered enough from your emotional challenges to engage with me?"

"I'm as steady as I can be. The wheels of industry must continue rolling. Our work here is important and I plan to use it to honor Eden's memory. What can I do for you?"

"How brave of you," Crestwater said as he found a seat across from Jack. "Well, Armin has not reported for work nor has he attempted to contact me with a suitable excuse. Both infractions are punishable by termination. Can you offer insight as to his tardiness?"

"I can and I apologize for my oversight. Armin suffered a broken leg early this morning after the national address. He said he was so upset by the news that he wandered from his home and slipped on some ice on his front porch."

"I see," Crestwater began. "I must admit, I hadn't expected such an emotional response from our team. It fills me with hope to observe your loyalty. Dare I say you're all one step closer to pledging said loyalty through the 85LP?"

"You may. We've been discussing doing just that. We've come to realize that our resistance may be caused by misguided beliefs of a bygone era. We've recognized that true patriotism means trusting your government, following their guidance, and being the cure, not the virus."

"Impressive that you've found these truths of your own volition. Even more impressive, you've led our team into the light. Understand, I will continue to treat Willis with skepticism and keep him at a safe distance. I'm sure he will soon witness the enlightenment of his peers and join us in our fight during these troublesome times."

You're a dick. "I'm sure he will. I'll continue to work with him, but you may be surprised by the progress he's made. What's the other topic you wanted to discuss?"

"Oh, yes, forgive me. I'm so enamored with your change of heart, I nearly forgot." Crestwater struck a solemn tone as he continued. "I'm afraid it's about your former dwelling. I received news of its destruction. I was to gain access to it this week. The Bureau of Equitable Housing assigned it to me. However, it appears it had become the focus of a rogue group of BHR agents. They were executing an unauthorized search when a natural gas leak caused a catastrophic explosion that destroyed the entire dwelling and damaged several neighboring dwellings."

After his wave of panic subsided, Jack bit down on his anger. What was *equitable* about Crestwater being given Jack's home?

"I'm sorry to hear that you've lost your dwelling. I'm grateful you weren't injured. Stinger Machinery needs you. Tell me, were any of my neighbors hurt? Do you know what caused the leak? I left that dwelling in pristine condition."

"Thankfully, your neighbors were unscathed. The agents, however, were killed. Such goes the life of rogues. Nevertheless, please make yourself available for questioning. The Bureau of Equitable Housing has assigned a team of investigators. I told them you had nothing to do with the tragedy, but our government is forever thorough and will contact you directly. I'm sure their focus will be more on why the BHR targeted you. Just a formality, nothing to fret over."

Jack released the breath he'd been holding and gave a thankful nod as Crestwater stood to leave.

"Oh, Jack," Crestwater said as he reached the threshold to Jack's office. "We've been tasked with inspecting a sampling of rifles. Seems the CS has experienced a rash of malfunctions. I'm assuming we're being asked to perform the inspections due to our superior manufacturing process. I suggest we team your Neanderthal-ish uncle with a member of the Bureau of Equitable Labor Distribution for the inspections. Should be fun watching them work together."

Jack grinned. "Should be. Let me know when the samples arrive."

Chapter 7

9 a.m., January 3rd, Cleveland CS Headquarters

Billy listened to the chaos filtering into his office. From the sounds of it, the entire Citizen Soldier force was now on active duty. He wasn't surprised. Hell, he was responsible for part of it. He was on edge and exhausted, though. The bits and pieces of conversations he'd picked up since arriving were concerning. The CS was planning a blitzkrieg-style assault on his city. Why Captain Smith hadn't talked to him about the plan worried him. Something was wrong.

He'd also caught Thatcher glaring at him several times and he knew what was coming. The little shit had put the pieces together much faster than he'd expected. When he looked up from the mountain of Form 85EA-Emergency Activation forms, he found Smith in his doorway.

"Captain Smith," Billy said as he stood to greet his CO. "Looks like we're getting ready to storm the beaches. Is there something I should know?"

Smith entered Billy's office, shutting the door behind him. "Can you tell me what these are?" Smith asked as he set two M4 firing pins on Billy's desk.

"Um, those are firing pins, but I'm guessing you already know that. So, what's your question?"

Smith didn't appreciate Billy's tone. "Don't be a smart ass, Sergeant. You know what I'm asking!"

Billy knew but hadn't anticipated this happening and was stalling for time. "Sir, I assure you, I have no idea what your question is. Can you clarify?"

Smith jumped, his cell buzzing in his cargo pocket. A second later, he was grinning at the screen. "I have a pressing matter demanding my immediate attention. I'll be offline and offsite for the afternoon. You inspect those, closely. When I get back, you'll explain in detail what you've found. Until then, you're riding your desk." Smith turned to leave, stopping short of the door. "Keep that puke Albright busy. He's been … slacking off. I want him here a full eighteen hours. Ensure he carries his fair share of the workload and help him rededicate to the job. Have I made myself clear?"

"Crystal, sir."

Billy stared at the firing pins for a long minute. The difference between them was so subtle a simple visual inspection wouldn't cause suspicion. Someone had measured them.

The sound of a throat clearing pulled his attention to his office entrance. "Sergeant Ash, I need a word with you. The matter is pressing and requires privacy. Please join me outdoors; the crisp air will refresh our memories."

"Don't be an ass," Billy shot back. "And stop talking like a douche. It's annoying. I'm not freezing my balls off to listen to you drone on about something that will more than likely piss me off."

"Very well, but I'll be shutting your door as my topic implicates me. As an unwilling pawn in your cloak and dagger spy games, I aim to protect myself from its inevitable unraveling."

Billy ran a hand down his face, his frustration with Thatcher growing rapidly. "Sit and talk."

"Of course, sir. To ensure your understanding, I will speak as if addressing a five-year-old. I believe you to be guilty of treason. You used your position to blackmail me into supplying you with classified information. You then exploited said information to either assault the BHR headquarters directly or supplied it to others who then carried out the deadly attack. I'm here to offer you the opportunity to right that wrong, to turn yourself in."

"Huh. Big words coming from you, Thatcher. A soldier who aided and abetted defectors while hoarding food. Food that should've been distributed to the disadvantaged. You know, the people you claim to champion? You never returned it. Why?" Billy locked onto Thatcher's eyes, challenging him to press on.

"Ah, I assumed such a response. So predictable is the mind of an ingrate, it's almost laughable. I've weighed the outcomes. If I were to, say, provide Captain Smith with my notes from our meetings and beg his forgiveness, I'm confident he would show leniency for my devotion."

Billy regarded Thatcher. The lengthy silence rattled the smug little shit.

"Well, you've certainly boxed me in, haven't you?" Billy sighed, feigning defeat. "It appears I have no other options. I'm going to confess to Captain Smith when he returns. Seeing that I've caused you undue stress, I'm going to allow you to return the food, no questions asked. Go home, get the food, and return it here. I'll tell Smith it was my idea and I was using you to hoard food for my gain. I'll throw in that I exploited my position of authority …. You get the point. It'll also show the other CS that you're a man of integrity. I'll lie and tell him that I planted the BHR uniform in a sad attempt to blackmail you." Billy paused before forcing emotion into his voice and said, "Seems you've won our war. However, I feel honored to have lasted as long as I did against your superior intellect."

"It seems I have," Thatcher proclaimed triumphantly. "Don't feel ashamed. As you acknowledged, I'm of a superior intellect. Now, about your offer to return the food: Why do I feel you're being insincere? I'm sure it will require you to join me, at which point you'll execute me and possibly my family. Do you think me a fool?"

"I'm restricted to desk duty by Smith's order," Billy interrupted. "I'm stuck here until he returns. Seems my world is, as you say, unraveling. You're free to take one of the fleet cars or unused transports. Either way, you'll be alone. I'll grab the BHR uniform from my truck and turn it over when we're in front of the captain." Billy shook his head as he rubbed his eyes. "I can't believe I did this. I'm sorry, Thatcher. You deserved better, but I hope you understand I simply lost my way. I was simply trying to save Billson. Get moving. Smith should be back within the hour. Gives you barely enough time to get home and back. Then, we finally end this. It was good serving with you, soldier."

CHAPTER 8

9:22 A.M., TREMONT NEIGHBORHOOD, CLEVELAND, OHIO

Mathews read Billy's text twice before its significance materialized: It was a warning. A warning he'd ignore because he was going a bit stir-crazy. Plus, he was prepping his gear for the night ahead. Moving it to his basement—although probably a smart choice—wasn't something he was in the mood for.

Instead, he covered his equipment and perched in his second-story window, waiting to identify the reason Billy told him to take cover away from outside walls. Whatever it was, he figured it would be fun to watch.

The afternoon sun glinted off the fresh blanket of snow, hurting Mathew's eyes. Squinting through the glare, he focused on West 14th. Anything coming his way would come from 14th, and his second story gave him an unobstructed view.

After fifteen minutes, he'd grown bored, something that happened often and quickly these days. He grabbed his sat-phone and started composing a text to Billy when a silver sedan screeched to a stop in front of Thatcher's house. The sedan was identical to the one already parked in Thatcher's driveway. He hadn't noticed the other car arrive, but he knew who it belonged to.

When the driver's door finally swung open and Thatcher burst from the car, the pieces snapped together. This would end badly for everyone involved. He refocused on his sat-phone and texted a single word. "Intervene?"

He grinned as he read Billy's reply.

"Negative."

***

Thatcher stormed up his snow-covered walkway. *Why is a CS fleet car at my home? Did Billy dispatch a hit squad? Is my family already dead?* His thoughts spurred him forward as he drew his weapon and press-checked the Glock 17, ensuring a round was chambered.

Steps from his front door, he slid to a stop. He wasn't a fool. He'd enter through the rear of the dwelling, catching his would-be assassins by surprise. His excitement grew as he rounded the corner and raced toward the back door. *This is going to be glorious. I'll present the carcasses of Billy's henchmen to Captain Smith and gain my rightful place at his side.*

As he gripped the doorknob, Angus' tortured cries filtered through the door's single-pane window.

"I'm coming, my boy! Your father is here to save you," he whispered as he pushed into the kitchen. He followed the pistol clenched in his trembling hands through the kitchen and leaned against the wall to the side of the opening into the living room. Following his training, Thatcher cut the pie around the corner. The tactic kept most of his body shielded from hostile gunfire. He'd be able to engage the instant his Glock's sights found the enemy while presenting the smallest target possible. *You trained me well, Sergeant Ash. Sorry, I'll soon use that training to thwart your plans.*

Thatcher completed the sweep of the living room and found only his son standing in his playpen, screaming himself red-faced. He took a pensive step into the space then stopped. Straining to hear over Angus' wailing, he thought he heard a distant voice crying out to God.

Reality ripped through him. The voice belonged to Margaux. *They must be torturing her. That's the only explanation for her to beg a cartoon deity for mercy. I'm coming, my love! Stay strong!* He ran past his son, unconcerned with Angus' wellbeing, wholly focused on saving his wife.

Two steps at a time, Thatcher ascended to the second floor. Stopping on the landing, he steadied himself. He had to act decisively, not hesitating to end the lives of the person or persons Billy sent to persecute his beautiful family.

His thought was interrupted by what sounded like a bed's headboard banging against the wall followed quickly by Margaux once again pleading with a God she didn't believe in and his son.

Thatcher burst into his bedroom a flash later, his gun searching wildly for his wife's tormentors. His mind reeled. Clothing lay strewn about the room. A gun belt hung from the bed's footboard. His wife—his beautiful wife—was nude, kneeling on their bed while passionately kissing a man as he groped her porcelain skin. Margaux wasn't being tortured.

"What ... what's happening?" His voice scarcely loud enough to garner their attention. His blood turned icy as his tear-blurred vision cleared. He was staring into Captain Smith's smiling face.

"Put the gun away, douche. Watch how a real man works, it might save your marriage."

Margaux pushed at Smith as she wriggled, breaking free of his grasp. Leaping from the bed, she rushed toward her husband. "Thatcher, you must believe me! He forced himself upon me. I was powerless against him."

Thatcher's vision swam, the room tilting hard to the right. He fought to remain standing, to face reality. Hysterical laughter pulled his focus back to Smith, who was now standing.

"Powerless you were, but also more than willing," Smith goaded, the smug smile never leaving his face as he slowly dressed. "She begged for it, Thatch. Said she needed a real man. Needed to feel like a woman again. Said something about you … what was it you said, Margy? Oh, I remember. She said sleeping with you was like sleeping with a woman. Soft, *all over*."

Smith laughed as he lunged for his gun.

Chapter 9

9:33 A.M., January 3rd, Mathews' Home

Mathews dove to the floor after hearing the first shot. Dozens more followed in quick succession. From the sound, he determined two different caliber guns were firing indiscriminately.

He pulled his sat-phone and pounded out a text to Billy. "Shots fired, a lot of shots fired."

"I know." Billy's response confused Mathews.

How does he know? The thought no sooner formed when he heard tires screeching on pavement. He dared to get to all fours and peek over the windowsill. Billy was running towards Thatcher's house, gun drawn.

Mathews was on the move as soon as he saw Billy. The shooting had stopped, but with two gunmen in Thatcher's house, the odds were stacked against Billy. Mathews planned to even those odds.

Mathews secured his gun in his concealed waistband holster before grabbing a baseball bat. He was standing beside Billy on Thatcher's porch seconds later.

"I breach, you take point."

"Got it," Billy replied just before Mathews slammed his foot against the door. The door exploded inward two kicks later.

Billy charged into the house in a crouch while Mathews waited on the pouch.

"Clear," Billy yelled. "Be advised, we have an unattended child in the living room."

The men cleared the entire first floor with the efficiency of a top-tier tactical response team. The child's screams made it nearly impossible to hear, putting both men on edge.

Billy scooped the youngster from his playpen and quickly inspected him for wounds. "He's uninjured. Take him to your house, I'll clear the second floor."

Mathews took Angus from Billy's arms and bolted for the door, using his body to shield the child from any gunfire that may erupt.

Billy stood motionless, straining to hear. After a few seconds, sobbing and harsh whispers filtered to him from the second floor.

"This is Sergeant Billy Ash of the Cleveland Citizen Soldiers. I'm coming upstairs—do *not* shoot. I'm here to help. Is anyone hurt? Do you need an ambulance?"

Billy heard more harsh whispers, slightly louder this time, as he ascended the stairs. Sweat streaked the sides of his face as he made it to the second-floor landing.

"Does anyone require medical attention?"

"No, Sergeant Ash, an ambulance isn't necessary. You should, however, call the morgue. A party of one needs transportation." The voice belonged to Thatcher. His statement caused the sobbing to intensify. "Another matter to address, Sergeant, is how to deal with my whore wife. I'd appreciate your feedback." His words spat more than spoken.

OA: Consent of the Governed

The sobbing morphed into wailing as Billy rushed towards the room he determined Thatcher was in. The door stood half open, blocking his view of who was in the room and where they were located. Using his foot, he tapped it and waited for gunfire to erupt. When it didn't, he entered slowly with his gun leading the way.

"I assure you, Sergeant, your firearm isn't required. I'm surrendering to you of my own volition," Thatcher said as he tossed his pistol onto the bed, its slide locked back on an empty chamber.

Seventeen rounds? You put seventeen rounds into one man? Billy's thoughts were interrupted as Thatcher stepped to the bed and sat next to his empty Glock, revealing the crumpled body lying in a growing puddle of blood.

Billy scanned the room for threats before holstering his weapon. Smith—or the body he assumed to be Smith's—was most assuredly dead. By his estimate, Thatcher had sent at least half a magazine of 9mm rounds through his face. The other half riddled his chest. The walls were peppered with bullet holes and the air was thick with the haze of spent gunpowder.

Billy was perplexed. How in this tight space did Smith not hit Thatcher with a single round? The man still gripped a 1911 in his lifeless hand. Billy had seen him send thousands of rounds downrange. He never missed … not once.

Billy shook away his confusion. He'd achieved half of his goal. The other half sat on the bed staring blankly at the gun he'd used to inflict more damage on a human being than Billy had ever seen.

Margaux's blubbering had calmed to gasping sobs. The large welt covering half of her face was painful evidence that she had tried to stop her lover's slaughter. Billy watched as the welt took the form of a trigger guard and realized she'd been pistol-whipped.

"I would have shot her as well, but I ran out of ammunition." Thatcher's voice startled Billy. The scene had wholly distracted him.

"You would have regretted it." Billy picked up Thatcher's gun while keeping a cautious eye on Margaux. "Miss Fulbright, please hold this until I secure the room."

Margaux startled at her name being spoken, her face snapping in his direction. Appearing to act on instinct, she reached out and took the gun from Billy, grabbing it by the slide. "Is my son safe?"

Billy nodded. "He's safe. Do me a favor, hold the gun by its frame. If you release the slide, it'll slam on your fingers."

Margaux gave Billy a questioning stare.

"The part with the trigger attached to it. It's safer when you hold it that way."

He watched as she did exactly what he expected: gripped the gun while sliding her finger inside the trigger guard.

"That's better. I'm going to cover you up. I promise I won't make any sudden moves."

"The whore deserves no civility. Let the world see her for what she is," Thatcher mumbled absently.

"He forced himself on me. You must believe me. He was so powerful and large, I was unable to fend him off."

Billy noticed Margaux's lustful tone, her eyes glazing as if she were remembering a joyous event.

The inflection didn't escape Thatcher. "I hate you, you vile witch. Sergeant, please remove her from my presence. I'll not be responsible for my actions if she remains in this room."

"Look, both of you, we have a situation here," Billy chided as he covered Margaux with a blanket. "It's far more pressing than your failed marriage. A government official is dead, killed by one of you. We need to determine who killed him and why. And we need to do it before anyone else arrives."

Thatcher turned to face his sergeant, his eyes searching for Billy's meaning.

"I didn't see what happened. It could be a case of self-defense when a jealous lover broke into your house and attacked you. Or, maybe, Smith tried to break things off with your wife and she experienced a mental breakdown, grabbed your gun, and, well, you know the rest. Could be a lot of things. But my gut tells me you had nothing to do with it; you're the victim, Thatcher. Of that, I'm sure."

Billy glanced at Margaux. His words elicited no response. Maybe she hadn't heard him or didn't understand his implications. She simply stared at the gun resting in her lap while quietly sobbing.

"Thatcher," Billy said. "Are you carrying any evidence bags?"

"I'm not. But I believe we have some food storage bags in the kitchen. Will they suffice?"

Billy nodded. "Get me six or seven ... actually, bring the entire box."

When Thatcher returned, he found Margaux zip-cuffed and lying face down on the bed, struggling to free herself. Billy stood when Thatcher entered the room. He'd slipped his pinky finger into the Glock's mag-well. He motioned for Thatcher to open a bag and slid the gun in.

"We can't have her fingerprints getting smudged. What's our next move, Thatcher?"

Thatcher understood his sergeant's meaning and was content to let this play out. "I believe page three, section four-A of the CS rule book is clear on this matter. She is to be taken into custody, placed in central holding where she will await sentencing. No trial necessary in cases involving the death of government officials."

"Are you insane?" Margaux screamed. "I had nothing to do with this! I tried to intervene, pushed Russell's gun away, saving your pathetic life. Look around you! If not for me, those bullet holes in our walls would be in your flimsy, worthless body. I demand to be freed, cut loose of these shackles! You are violating the Fourteenth Amendment. I have rights!"

"Shut up, you insufferable hag," Thatcher interrupted. "You have no *rights* when a government official is murdered. The laws have changed, my dear."

To escape Margaux's earsplitting protest, Billy led Thatcher into the hall and shut the door behind him.

Thatcher regarded Billy with suspicion. "After everything I've done to you, you could easily, and justifiably, lock me away forever. I killed a man, an officer of the Citizen Soldiers. What do you want? What will this cost me?"

A crooked grin creased Billy's features. "I'm looking out for my soldiers. It's what we do. We take care of our own. As for the cost, we'll talk about that later. Right now, I'm giving you three minutes alone with your wife. Say your goodbyes."

Thatcher tried to ask another question, but Billy waved him away as he grabbed his radio. "This is Sergeant Ash. We have a man down … Captain Smith is dead, murdered by Margaux Fulbright. Dispatch a squad to Private Fulbright's dwelling. Suspect secured, no ambulance required." Billy reattached his radio to its shoulder mount and locked Thatcher in a hard stare. "Give me your phone."

Thatcher quickly complied. He flinched when Billy slammed it to the floor, then stomped it to tiny shards.

"Your phone got smashed after you called me for help. You came home early. Found your wife in bed with Smith. She had a mental breakdown, went into a blind rage, took your gun, and tried to shoot you. Smith attempted to stop her and she unloaded your pistol into him. It all happened so fast, it's just a blur. It's okay to cry. You're distraught; the woman you love killed the man you admired most. Repeat that until you believe it. Until it's true. If you do, you'll have nothing to worry about."

Thatcher nodded. His calm acceptance of the story—of the whole damn situation—sent a chill through Billy.

"Three minutes, then we talk about your future. Oh, one last thing: I *will* gut you if you screw this up."

Chapter 10

10 a.m., January 3rd, Command Center

"Jesus, Joseph, and Mary, you stink. Mathews, why does this kid smell so bad? What are they feeding him?" Lisa held Angus with stiff arms, her nose crinkled in disgust. "Seriously, I thought you guys were joking or exaggerating, but holy shit. He's like a tiny stink bomb. Take him back. I don't think he's cute anymore. Actually, get him out of here. This is where I live. I can't have it smelling like baby poop."

Mathews retreated to the furthest point in the room. "No. The little rat probably needs his diaper changed which is something I'm not equipped to do. Change it and I'll take him to my house."

"Change him? With what? I don't have any diapers or baby wipes and I'm sure as hell not tossing his dirty diaper into my trash. Take him, now!"

"No! I thought women were nurturing, always prepared to take care of a child? I got him out of that house. My job is done."

Lisa glared at Mathews, her stare so intense he turned his back to her. "Your female intimidation tactics won't work!"

"Poop!" Angus squealed.

"You can talk? Why didn't you tell us that sooner?" Lisa asked the giggling child. "Can you change yourself?"

"POOP!"

"Mathews, his vocabulary is on par with yours. Take him. He's getting heavy. Take him and I won't beat you senseless for being an ass. If you don't, I'll demonstrate exactly how un-nurturing I can be."

Mathews didn't move a muscle or respond. Instead, he simply stared at the wall of guns in front of him and tried to focus on their inherently beautiful forms.

"Look, you dumb shit. I have to monitor what's happening outside. If we end up with a bunch of CS crawling up our asses, I'm going to tell UW it happened because you were afraid to touch a baby."

"Turn on one of the radios we took from the BHR agents. You should be able to monitor their coms. We'll know exactly what they're doing." Mathews paused, then proudly exclaimed, "Checkmate!"

Lisa stormed in Mathews' direction and set Angus at his feet. On her way back to her workstation, she addressed Mathews over her shoulder. "Do you pay attention during our weekly calls? Don't answer that. Clearly, you don't. We can't use the radios until we figure out if they have tracking devices in them. Billy doesn't know if they do, so I removed their batteries until I determine if activating them will bring the BHR to our doorstep." Lisa grinned as she retook her position in front of her workstation. "Tell you what, you take one of them to your house *with* Angus. Turn it on and listen real close to what's going on. Then, report your findings. I'm curious to know what the enlightenment camps are like … oh, maybe you'll get assigned to the Mojave camp! No more winters for you."

"Poop," Angus screeched as he pulled himself up using Mathews' leg.

"That was wrong on so many levels. How does Jack live with you? And I'll have you know I listen *and* participate during our calls. But, sometimes, you drone on for hours and hours and I nod off. That's probably when you told us about the radios."

"Holy shit," Lisa said. "What the hell happened over there?"

Mathews caught the urgency in her voice. She wasn't talking about stinky diapers. He moved to join her, forgetting Angus had leeched to his pants, and nearly fell when the child's weight dragged his leg to a stop.

"Damn it, kid. Sit your stinky butt here and don't move," he said as he set Angus in the middle of Lisa's bed. He waited a second to ensure he wouldn't squirm off the edge, then rushed to join Lisa.

Mathews sucked in a sharp breath. He hadn't seen a more impressive show of force since his time in the sandbox.

"I figured it was serious, but this," he said, pointing at the screen, "is overkill. We're talking about one or two armed suspects, tops. I'm sure Thatcher took the brunt of it. What are they saying?"

"I don't know, they're out of range for our microphones. It's just a bunch of garbled voices."

The duo watched, searching the crowd for Billy. Neither had expressed it, but both were worried. The situation with Thatcher and his wife was volatile. Give Thatcher a gun and anything was possible.

Mathews was brutally aware of the statistics surrounding domestic violence calls. More importantly, how the person intervening often became the focus of the victim's rage. The police department shrinks had a name for it. Mathews simply called it painful. It was the reason he sported a scar over his left eye. If the woman responsible had been holding a gun instead of a beer bottle, he'd be dead, and her boyfriend would have finished beating her senseless.

Several minutes ticked by with no sign of Billy. Mathews noticed the Citizen Soldiers' lack of discipline. There was no security perimeter, and some were huddled into tight groups. Others were trying to force their way into Thatcher's home, creating a bottleneck ripe for an ambush.

"I could kill half of them in under a minute. Do you think UW would green-light an impromptu assault?"

"I agree, but not a chance he lets *us* do it. Asking will just piss him off."

Lisa watched the monitor while trying to adjust the microphones. It was no use. "What we need to ask UW for is a solid tech guy—someone talented enough to get us deeper into the BHR system, scan the radios for tracking devices, and figure out how to create essential badges. Me scanning a bunch of BHR emails isn't effective or a long-term solution."

"There," Mathews shouted while pointing at the monitor's upper right-hand corner. "That's Billy! Thatcher's right behind him." He waited a tick, then realized what he was seeing. "We've got a body bag. Holy shit, they've got Margaux cuffed."

As they watched, Billy glanced in the camera's direction and held up his gov-issued phone.

"I think that's for you," Lisa said. "Grab Stinky and get out of here. Make sure you're outside before you call him."

"Got it," Mathews barked as he snatched Angus from her bed.

Chapter 11

11:59 p.m., January 3rd, Command Center, Willis Stinger's Home

Lisa watched as Willis worked through his options. The neighborhood was still crawling with CS. Dozens of them patrolled the surrounding streets, randomly searching homes, and dragging people into the brisk evening air to question them. The spectacle was meant to instill fear and elicit cooperation.

"You're sure nothing else happened today? Just the shitshow at Thatcher's?"

"That's all I noticed, but we're pretty limited. I've seen nothing to indicate another incident in the BHR email traffic, but that doesn't mean much." Lisa had answered that question three times but considering Willis' mood, she opted not to complain.

"Jack, contact Randy and Armin. Ask them if the same thing is happening to them. I'll call Callahan. Lisa, contact Texas and text Mathews; tell him he's on Wyoming. We need to determine if this is localized or national."

Within minutes, they had their answer: It was local to Cleveland Metro. The national response to Eden's assassination proved more subdued through a simple show of force. The room deflated. They'd been gearing up for the night ahead. They had targets identified and a solid tactical plan in place.

"Damn Thatcher," Willis barked.

Jack glanced at his gear. He'd been looking forward to this more than he realized. He took it as a good sign. He was coming to grips with his new reality, no doubt helped by Lisa's words.

"UW, maybe we can salvage the night. We won't be able to hit our planned targets, but we have a bunch walking the streets right outside our front door."

Willis turned to face Jack, features vacillating between shock and pride. "Get Mathews on speakerphone."

2:01 a.m., January 4th

"I'm telling you," Mathews whispered. "The kid's shit was bright green. I've never smelled anything so nasty. Thatcher blamed the avocados they feed him, but his rat child has always stunk. I think it's genetics. Bad genetics."

"Why'd you wait around?" Jack asked. "I would have dropped the brat and ran. Once he was with his dad, you were off the hook. I mean, Billy slipped you the keys to Captain Smith's car. You were babyless and the place was swarming with CS. Staying to watch him change a diaper makes zero sense."

Willis had been listening to their banter since they'd taken cover behind a dumpster after a CS Armored Personnel Carrier blasted down the street, narrowly missing them with its spotlight.

The CS patrols had thinned as the night turned to early morning. At 0130, Willis gave the order to move out. The plan was simple: travel roughly six blocks east to the corner of West 7th and Jefferson, isolate a small CS patrol, engage, and return home. Lisa was monitoring the area immediately surrounding their house and would advise them if their return path was clear.

The CS uniforms Billy had supplied made for relatively uneventful travel. Willis understood that with light infantry weapons, they were no match for an APC if things went sideways. Their ballistic vests weren't rated to stop 30-cal rounds, so he chose the better part of valor and ordered them to take cover.

"He did it because he's ex-Army. A Marine would've made sure the child was safe, accepted the keys to an extremely valuable asset, and double-timed back to base. He would *not* have jeopardized the operation by watching a man change diapers. That, Jack, is the difference between a Marine and everybody else."

"You Stingers are a nasty clan. Especially after I saved your asses when two poorly trained, overweight, mentally challenged government lackeys caught you flatfooted in your own house …. So sad."

Willis raised a fist, silencing them. A tick later, he held up three fingers. Jack and Mathews readied to engage three Citizen Soldiers. Willis spun a finger over his head. They were standing on the street in an instant.

"They're too far away. Let them close on us," UW whispered.

The three-man patrol was at thirty yards and closing on their position. As they passed through the cones of light thrown from the streetlamps, Jack noticed their guns. "MP5s. We've got a BHR patrol."

"Even better," Mathews sneered while tightening his grip on his suppressed M4.

"The government isn't paying you boys to stand around. Move your asses." It was the largest of the BHR patrol barking at them. His voice rang familiar to Jack.

"That was an order!" The man yelled when none of them moved.

"Relax," UW shot back. "We have questions. Hoped you'd have answers. Like, why the hell we're still on patrol, freezing our balls off when the killer's already in custody and the area's secured?"

The BHR patrol was closing fast and Willis' question accelerated their pace. At ten feet, Jack figured it out. "Sampson, is that you? When'd they pull you off food-distro?"

Sampson's eyes narrowed as his head tilted. "I've been off distribution for months. If we're friends, you'd know that."

"Who said we're friends?" Jack's voice was low and menacing.

Sampson stepped quickly towards Jack when two suppressed rounds unexpectedly ripped through his leg, sweeping it from under his bulk and crashing him to the pavement. Time stopped. None of them had fired on Sampson.

The wounded agent screamed and clutched his leg, breaking their trance and causing his squad to spin wildly, searching for the shooter. UW knelt, unsure if Sampson was the sniper's intended target or the unfortunate recipient of poorly aimed rounds meant for Jack.

UW used the confusion and quickly sent three rounds into the trailing agent, ensuring he wouldn't escape into the dark. He adjusted his aim, centering his red dot on the standing agent's chest. The man's eyes went wide, and he brought his MP5 to firing position. His body jerked violently three, then four times.

5.56 rounds slammed into his chest and sent him stumbling backward, his arms flailing, trying to regain balance.

"Down," UW yelled a split second before the agent's MP5 rattled to life, spraying errant rounds in every direction.

Jack realized what had happened when he heard a deep thump and air rushing from Mathews' lungs. He hadn't moved fast enough and crumpled to the ground, landing next to Jack.

"I'm hit," Mathews wheezed, his voice raspy and strained. "That little fucker shot me."

"Did it punch through your vest?"

"Don't know, Jack, but it sure as hell feels like I have some broken ribs. Damn, does this hurt."

"Stay low," UW shouted. "We don't know if the sniper's friendly."

"Mathews was hit. We need to move, *now*."

"Where? How bad?" UW asked as he crawled past Jack toward Mathews.

"Chest. Don't know," Jack answered, then turned to Mathews. His friend's face twisted in agony. "We need to roll, A-SAP."

"Bullshit. You need to call a medevac. I'm bleeding out," Sampson bellowed, appearing unaware of what had transpired.

Jack's head snapped in Sampson's direction. The man lay five feet away, writhing on the frosty pavement. He rolled to his side and met Jack's glare. "I said call a medevac! Are you fucking deaf?"

Jack surged toward Sampson, army-crawling as swiftly as if he were walking. "You haven't figured it out, have you? You're going to die. You should know something before you go: We also have eyes everywhere."

Recognition flashed across Sampson's face. Jack smiled as he unsheathed his K-Bar. "We're taking it back." He slammed the knife through Sampson's temple before the man could react.

As Jack re-sheathed his knife, UW said, "I've got Mathews; you're on point." He was already standing and supporting Mathews.

Jack was on his feet in a flash. He turned in a slow circle, trying to identify the path they'd taken. His confusion cleared as the adrenaline slowly bled from his system. He took a step and stopped, recalling the direction from which the rounds had slammed into Samson's leg. If he continued, he'd be leading them in that very direction.

"We need to find another route. If the shooter isn't friendly, we'll be perfect targets."

"We don't have time," UW said. "Plus, we'd already be dead if he was hostile. Move!"

Trusting UW's instincts, Jack set course for home, his rifle tracking left to right and his finger resting on its trigger. He'd decided to shoot anything that moved.

Chapter 12

2:20 a.m., January 4th, Randy's Home

Initially furious, Randy eventually calmed. He understood why Willis had ordered him to stand down. The city was crawling with Citizen Soldiers; they would have intercepted him the second he stepped outside. If the CS connected the dots, his arrest could have jeopardized the entire mission.

He'd watched nervously as several of his neighbors were forced from their homes, interrogated and some arrested. After several hours, he realized the Citizen Soldiers were avoiding his home. He didn't understand why but chose not to question his good fortune.

The upside was being left behind allowed him to focus on his projects. He'd be a liability if he didn't develop a communication system when they were on a mission. The IX operation had proved it. Willis had assigned him to guard the transport because he wouldn't be able to hear commands.

More pressingly, the Bureau of Harm Reduction, in conjunction with the Bureau of Equitable Labor Distribution, had already placed a sign-reader with Stinger Machinery. Randy believed the next government serf would possess the ability as well. It was only a matter of time until their signed conversations were no longer private.

To combat their efforts, Randy had begun developing a unique version of sign language weeks earlier. Through a combination of SEE (Signing Exact English) the form they currently used, with Aslan (Australian Sign Language) and defaulting to the BSL's (British Sign Language) two-handed alphabet for specific words, he'd devised a basic yet effective new dialect. He felt confident that, if occasionally tweaked, it would conceal their conversations from prying eyes. After all, he had one hundred and forty-two different sign languages to choose from.

He'd spent the last two weeks developing a guide and would distribute it tomorrow during lunch. He crossed his fingers the team would accept his idea as he clicked the print command.

After assembling the freshly printed guides, he'd texted Lisa for updates. The team hadn't checked in. His anxiety was building. He considered setting out to search for them but shook the thought away. Lisa promised she'd update him when she had information.

After several laps around his living room trying to burn off his nervous energy, Randy headed for the basement. It was time to revisit his second project.

He resecured the wall panel, sealing the recess where he hid his gear and other valuables, and set the foam-padded black case on his workbench. This was his only hope for remaining an active member of the team.

Within minutes, Randy was maneuvering the Mavic Pro Platinum ultra-quiet drone through his multi-roomed basement, testing it when it was out of his line of sight, adjusting the video feed, and practicing touch and go landings. His skills were improving. Actually, he was pretty damn good at piloting it. Randy knew he'd eventually perform real-world testing but hadn't wanted to risk it. His trepidation had passed.

The drone would have been perfectly suited for their IX Center mission. He could have cut their anxiety levels by identifying the gunshots and the approaching diesel engine. Both had proved inconsequential, just BHR soldiers ripping through the parking lot in a Humvee shooting at shadows. But, God forbid if the agents had spotted them. He could have charted a path to safety or set up an ambush. The tactical advantages were endless.

He'd synced the drone with an older unused Samsung S8 when he bought it two years ago. At the time, it was a novelty. After a couple of weekends zipping around the Metro Parks, he stored it away and kicked himself for spending north of eight hundred dollars on it. Ultimately, he shrugged off the expense. With no one but himself to spend his money on, the drone was merely one of countless impulse buys he'd made over the years.

He considered sending it to scan the area around Willis' home, but at ten miles, it was just outside the drone's range. Instead, he decided to test it in his neighborhood. His research indicated the drone was ultra-quiet, emitting only sixty decibels of sound. Being deaf, he couldn't be positive and had to trust what he'd read.

Tonight's the night. His thought brought a smile to his face while his stomach flipped with a mixture of anticipation and fear. Strapping his Sig P320 to his side and covering it with his flannel, he rushed upstairs with his drone in hand.

Chapter 13

3:31 a.m., January 4th, Willis Stinger's Home

UW laid Mathews on Lisa's bed and ripped the side-mounted hook and loop fasteners of his Kevlar vest free.

"This'll probably hurt," UW said before pulling the vest over Mathews' head.

"A Marine would probably cry, but not an Army gru—Holy shit, UW! Are you trying to kill me?" Mathews yelled as UW peeled the vest from his heavily bruised and swollen skin.

Jack would have sworn the multicolored contusion was growing as he watched Mathews squirm, trying to escape the pain. His eyes frantically searched his friend's chest for signs of an entry wound, but the massive, quickly darkening bruise made it difficult to discern healthy skin from a ragged hole. A moment later, Jack noticed a thin trickle of blood escaping Mathews' crowning wound.

"Shit," he whispered as he locked eyes with UW.

"Shit? What shit? Why did you say shit?" Mathews asked as his head swiveled between Jack and UW, searching for an answer.

"Relax," UW said, his voice even and calm before holding up two mushroomed bullets. "They didn't penetrate, but you definitely have at least one broken rib, probably more. We need to ice your chest before the swelling rips you wide open."

"He needs a doctor," Lisa interjected. "Without x-rays, we won't know if his ribs splintered. If they did, they could puncture his lungs or worse."

"Or worse?" Mathews yelled. "What worse? How much worse? Someone answer my damn questions!"

UW glared at Lisa. He understood she was trying to help, but she should have been more selective with her phrasing. She nodded in response and turned back to her monitors.

"We're going to ice it and pump you full of painkillers. Then, we'll figure out how to get you to the hospital without raising suspicion."

"I've got an idea," Lisa said from her workstation. "But he won't like it."

Chapter 14

7:33 a.m., January 4th, IX Center, Cleveland Ohio

Agent in Command Wolfe stormed through the IX Center's chilled interior, offering blistering commentary to any agent unfortunate enough to cross his path. They'd passed the forty-eight-hour mark since the attack and were still without power. The hum of four emergency generators—a sound he'd quickly learned to hate—never stopped. If not for the scant amount of power they supplied, he'd have ordered them destroyed.

The news, delivered by an agent he'd reduced to tears, was the catalyst for his tantrum. Repairs could take two to three weeks. The cause of the delay proved the same as every other shortage currently plaguing them: supply chain issues created by a lack of qualified workers capable of being granted essential status.

"We've got holding cells full of fresh detainees and three dead agents. We need power—*full* power. Not one of you worthless sons-a-bitches knows how to fix this!?" he screamed as he slammed the door to his office.

Seconds after taking his seat, a knock on his office door nearly ended with him shooting through it and killing whoever stood on the other side.

"If you can't fix the damn substation, you best leave!" Wolfe became incensed when the door opened.

"Agent in Command, I apologize for intruding." The voice belonged to Veronica Haze, his assistant, who wisely didn't enter his office. "I have a package from BHR headquarters in Washington, D.C. It's marked urgent and for your eyes only. Should I leave it here, in the hall?"

"Enter," Wolfe snapped.

Veronica pushed through the door, awkwardly wheeling the package next to Wolfe's desk on a dolly.

"What the hell is that? Why such a large box?"

Veronica shook her head. "Your eyes only, sir."

"Any luck with that name I gave you?" Wolfe replied, ignoring his oversight. "Bard, was it? Who the hell names their kid Bard?"

"Um, sir," Veronica said, eyes wide with fear. "Are you familiar with Dungeons and Dragons?"

Wolfe's confusion morphed into disgust. "You're telling me he was one of those sadomasochist sickos? More disturbing, he found people that willingly slept with him?"

"Sir, I—"

"And we're looking for one of his sicko sex *partners*?" Wolfe interrupted. "Or whatever you call them?"

"Sir!" Veronica interrupted. "Dungeons and Dragons is a role-playing game. Not a sadomasochist club."

Wolfe remained quiet, working through the information before blurting out his questions. "So, who's Bard? Should be easy enough to find, right? The company responsible for the game should have Bard's information. Get their contact info. I'll reach out directly."

"I'm not an expert, but what I've found …" Veronica paused, preparing herself for Wolfe's reaction. "Bard is a *class* of characters which live within the game."

Wolfe turned a shade of red Veronica had never seen. His reaction caused her to step back, creating distance between them.

"What the absolute fu—. You're kidding me!? How many Bard twits are there? Better question, what grown-ass man refers to his friends by the names assigned to them in a game? *Who*?"

Veronica flinched and closed her eyes as Wolfe's voice rose with each word. When the room fell silent, she quickly responded but kept her eyes shut tight. "Sir, it's an extremely popular game with millions of players. But—"

"Millions!" Wolfe bellowed. "How the hell do we find the person or persons Adam was talking about? *How*?"

"Sir, from what I've read, the players form small groups of five or six participants. We should be able to isolate his—his *group*, or whatever you'd call them, with relative ease."

The room was silent for a long minute, prompting Veronica to open her eyes. Wolfe locked her in a hard stare and she knew what it meant.

"Yes, sir. I'll get to work locating the players in Adam's group."

Veronica exhaled as she reached her desk and slouched into her chair. Overwhelmed by the task ahead of her, she rubbed at her temples, then suddenly looked at her monitor. Within seconds, she was scrolling through Adam's social media feeds.

Wolfe grabbed the box as Veronica exited. It was large and heavy, but oddly pliable. He ripped the packing tape free and pulled back the flaps. What he found confused him. Pulling several of the cloth-filled plastic-wrapped packages free, he eventually found what he was searching for: the Form 85EOS- Explanation of Shipment. "We used to call it a packing slip," Wolfe smirked while unfolding the document.

After a cursory review, things became clearer. The box held newly issued arm bands. The dark red bands with a black circle in the middle emblazoned with OA in white lettering were not to be issued until he received orders to do so.

His curiosity piqued, he reread the letter searching for clues as to the meaning of OA but found nothing.

He held a band up for inspection. Wolfe couldn't escape the feeling he'd seen them before. They were worryingly familiar. He slipped the cheaply made cloth over his left arm. After struggling with the elastic, he'd eventually positioned the band mid-bicep. He regarded it for a long minute before moving to the mirror hanging next to his coat rack.

Wolfe stared, disbelievingly, at his reflection. The image staring back sent a chill down his spine. He remembered where he'd seen the bands.

Chapter 15

2 p.m., January 4th, Command Center

Lisa held her sat-phone in one hand while pinching the bridge of her nose with the other. Billy was explaining what had happened at Thatcher's. It wasn't making things better.

"So, your plan was to either have them kill each other or—if they didn't—you'd kill them and stage it to look like they'd slaughtered one another in a wild shootout?"

"That was the plan," Billy replied. "Lisa, I nearly shit myself when I figured out what had happened. The chances of Thatcher taking Smith out were less than zero. He walked away without a scratch. It's impossible."

"I understand, but why isn't Thatcher dead? He's a liability! You should have killed him."

Billy paused. Lisa's sharp tone irked him. "I had seconds—less than seconds—to act," Billy shot back. "Lisa, tell me, what would you have done? Kill them all, including a baby? I'll work on Thatcher tomorrow. By the time I'm done, I'll have him pinned under my boot. He knows how it works. I saved his ass. He owes me. He'll fall back in line."

Lisa shook her head. UW was going to be furious when she told him. She sensed Billy's frustration and shifted the subject back to the M4s. "Alright, I'll brief Willis, but prepare for a call from him. Now, how did Smith figure it out? Measuring the firing pins should have never happened. At a glance, they're identical to an in-spec pin. I've inspected them myself. Someone must have used a dial-caliper. Maybe he did?"

Billy hadn't considered the *how*. Instead, he assumed Smith had stumbled onto it by accident. The implications were devastating.

"He was a marksman, used to prattle on about his accomplishments. We knew he could shoot. We'd all seen him blister targets with two-inch groups, but figured the rest was bullshit because he was always drunk when he launched into his stories. Meaning, he may have figured it out. More importantly, it shows he no longer trusted me. Someone was in his ear!"

"Have you seen that group he's been working with? The soldiers he's been giving extra attention to?" Lisa interrupted.

"They haven't been at HQ in weeks. With Smith dead, I have no idea what they'll be doing."

"You need to find out quickly. The last thing we need is a CS special op's team roaming the streets."

Billy heard bits and pieces of what Lisa said. His attention was drawn to the sedan pulling to a stop in Smith's designated parking space. The car itself was unspectacular. However, the flags affixed to its hood were startling. Each displayed a stylized eagle, its talons gripping a single star.

Billy recalled the video footage of Eden's body swinging from Mount Weather's flagstaff. Below his shriveled form, dancing lazily in the soft breeze, flew this exact flag. His gaze broke as three of the car's doors swung open.

Billy, so distracted by the vehicle and the men exiting it, had forgotten about Lisa and, more recklessly, the sat-phone pressed to his ear.

"I've got to go," he whispered as he disconnected the call and dropped the phone to his truck's floorboard. Using his feet, he slid it into the hidden compartment and kicked the floor mat into place.

The trio, dressed in standard-issue gray BDUs, had taken notice and began walking in his direction. Billy realized if he was questioned, he could offer no reason for sitting in his truck in the middle of the day. Pretending to be concentrating on something in his lap, he kept his head down, avoiding eye contact. He pulled out his gov-issued cell and quickly reinserted its battery.

The trio was mere feet from his truck as he dialed his dad's number, hit send, and put him on speaker. "Hey, dad. Just checking in, it's been a while."

A slap on the driver's side window interrupted his father's reply. Billy snapped his head to face the visitor and attempted to look startled by the intrusion.

"Exit the vehicle, immediately." The man's heavy accent rendered him barely understandable.

Billy held up his phone, showing him he was on a call, and motioned he'd need another minute.

"Now!" the man yelled as he slapped the window, then attempted to yank open the locked door. "This instant, you will exit the vehicle or we will drag you out."

Billy, shocked by the man's caustic reaction, started when a second man began pounding on the passenger side window. "Dad, I've gotta go. Three angry Asian men want to talk to me. I'll call you later."

Billy's door was yanked open the instant he unlocked it. "Show me your badge. Why are you sitting in your car? Are you a Citizen Soldier? You should be at your workstation. Lazy Americans—can't count on any of you to perform your assigned duties."

Billy, positioned with one leg in and one out of the truck, regarded the man. Sharply pressed pants tucked tight inside gleaming regulation boots. His captain bars were pinned to his BDU blouse's collar, its orientation exactly as the rule book dictated. The flag patch on his right shoulder grabbed Billy's attention: an eagle grasping a star.

"Excuse me, sir, but who are you?" Billy said as he slid from the truck and presented his badge. "We've received intel that imposters may have infiltrated our ranks, so I'll need to see your badge."

The slightly built, vertically challenged man glared at Billy but he understood Billy was following protocol and snatched his badge from his neck and shoved it in Billy's face.

"Captain Yang Wei. It's good to meet you, sir. I'm Sergeant Billy Ash, Cleveland Citizen Soldiers. How may I assist you and your team?"

"Are you a smart ass, Sergeant *Billy Ash*? You strike me as such. Remain silent and listen carefully. I'm assuming command of this facility and its force."

One of Yang's team yelled something in Mandarin, cutting the captain off. It startled Billy when Yang spun to face the man, then slapped him. "Never interrupt me again."

Yang turned back to Billy. Taking a menacing step, he closed the gap between them to mere inches. "Sergeant, the next time you disobey a direct order, you will be relieved of your position.

You will not receive such leniency a third time. Do I make myself clear?"

"Yes, sir. I hope the captain understands my hesitancy to respond to your commands. I received no official notification of your arrival. My apologies, sir!"

Yang appeared placated by Billy's response, especially his apology. He turned to his team and said something in Mandarin, eliciting roaring laughter.

Billy ignored them and stifled his anger. "Would you like me to introduce you to your Citizen Soldier team, sir?"

"What an ignorant question from one responsible for the leadership of our troops. Of course, I want you to introduce me. Please, after you." Yang stepped aside and motioned for Billy to lead them into the building.

Billy watched, dumbfounded, as Yang exploded into the workspace the instant Billy finished speaking, slamming empty chairs to the floor and upending tables. The captain's team, whose names Billy learned while introducing them—Bai Guang and Fan Hao—were busy hurling the contents of every desk skyward. None of them spoke. They simply launched into a shotgun-style rampage that showed no signs of ending.

It became clear to Billy that they intended to intimidate and establish their dominance. It was working.

Maybe getting rid of Smith wasn't my best move. Billy thought as Yang came to a stop.

"You idiots are pathetic, unworthy of your positions. You call yourselves soldiers?" he yelled as he circled the area slowly, air pumping through flared nostrils. "Look at this place. It's disgusting! A mess. You have five minutes to bring this office to regulation. If you are unclear on what that means, we have no use for you; turn your equipment over to your sergeant and vacate the premises."

An awkward silence fell over the soldiers. They stood stock-still, fearing another scathing outburst from their new captain. Yang's eyes narrowed as he glared at his soldiers.

"I apologize. I forgot I'm dealing with Americans who must be led by the hand like monkeys at the zoo. Move *now!*"

Yang's words set off a flurry of activity as the soldiers rushed to meet the tyrant's demands. Billy shook his head as he watched the chaos. None of them took a leadership role with each focused solely on self-preservation. They'd missed the point: if one failed, they all failed.

Billy stepped toward the fray, intending to organize their efforts when Yang appeared in his path. "Sergeant Ash, join me in my office."

Shouting at Bai and Fan to supervise, Yang turned sharply toward the hallway where the leadership offices were located. As they traversed the mess, Billy locked eyes with Thatcher and gave a slight nod, which Thatcher returned. The man seemed unfazed, almost defiant, as he calmly worked to reorganize his workstation.

As Billy crossed the threshold of Yang's office, he heard a voice shouting orders and taking control. The realization stunned him. The voice belonged to Thatcher Fulbright.

Chapter 16

2:37 p.m., January 4th, Mathews' Home

Mathews had been sitting pin-straight on his recliner for hours. Afraid to move, he remained perfectly still, trying to avoid aggravating his broken rib. He'd taken three Vicodin over the eleven hours since Willis had deposited him in his chair. Now with two pills remaining, he debated between taking them both in hopes he'd overdose and end his suffering or waiting until Lisa's horrible plan dictated he take them.

He stuffed his hand between the seat cushions, stopping twice to let the pain subside before finally freeing his satellite phone. Now, he realized, he had a difficult choice: ignore the listening devices in his home and call Lisa on speaker or endure the pain of lifting the phone and composing a text. Either way, he intended to beg her to take him to a hospital A-SAP.

"Now?" he texted, after clearing his mind enough to realize that a call would bring the BHR to his doorstep.

He grimaced as he read her curt reply. "No. Stop texting. I'm busy!"

Mathews waited ninety seconds and sent another text. "Now?"

"I'm on my way." Her text sent waves of relief through him until he received her next message. "With a baseball bat. A broken leg and broken ribs will be more believable. See you in five."

Her third text, he felt, was unnecessarily cruel. "If you don't stop, I'll tell one of the fifty or so BHR agents on 7th you're the one that killed the agents."

"Nasty Stingers," was all he could muster. He hit send and began the painful process of hiding the phone between the cushions.

He decided to try distracting himself from the all-consuming pain and reached for the remote resting on his lap. The action released a bolt of pain so intense his vision dimmed as his consciousness faltered.

Mathews waited a full ten minutes before trying again, this time moving much slower, and finally found the power button. The talking head filling his screen was polling a panel of experts. Her query: the toll of Eden's assassination on the free world.

The voices faded. Mathews thought the mixture of opiates and pain was causing hallucinations, but they weren't. The writing, scrolling vertically on his television, was Chinese.

Chapter 17

2:47 p.m., January 4th, Cleveland Citizen Soldiers HQ

Yang slammed a folder onto his desk, then glared at Billy. "This is your personnel file, Sergeant Ash. Captain Smith spoke highly of you. After observing you for a short time, I do *not* share his sentiment. However, at this moment, your lack of professionalism is unimportant. According to Smith's calendar, you were scheduled to meet with him yesterday. He marked the meeting 'urgent, must attend.' What was this *urgent* meeting's topic?"

Billy held Yang's gaze as he spoke. "You'd have to ask him. All I know is he wanted to meet with me. I wasn't aware he'd even put it on his calendar or that it was urgent. He simply told me to hang around until he returned."

"Why, Sergeant Ash, do I think you're lying? I'll tell you why. You're asking me to believe that your commanding officer just casually asked you to *hang around*. Did he do this often? Because everything I've read about Captain Smith indicates he would not have been so informal."

Billy could barely understand Yang, his accent so thick he only understood every second word. They'd been at this less than five minutes and Billy was already exhausted from concentrating. He realized Yang would use the language barrier to his advantage.

"Sir, if I understand your question, you're asking me to speculate on Captain Smith's intentions—something I'm unwilling to do."

Yang recoiled at Billy's use of the word *understand*. "So, you dislike Chinese people? Asian hate is something I thought dwelled below CS standards. I'm even more disappointed in you, Sergeant Ash."

"Sir, I'll ask you to explain your assumptions," Billy responded, choosing his words carefully. "Specifically, what I said that led you to the conclusion I dislike Chinese or any Asian cultures?"

Yang regarded Billy, his eyes narrowed with suspicion. "It's not for you to question; you simply follow orders. You've dug yourself a deep hole, one for which your ladder is woefully insufficient."

Billy moved to end the interrogation before he lost his temper. "Sir, I believe I've answered your questions and have done so honestly. If you have no further inquiries regarding Captain Smith, I respectfully request to be dismissed."

Yang leaned his chair back while shaking his head, his disgust for Billy pure and unveiled. "You ask nothing. You speak when spoken to! I'll decide when our meeting is over. Obviously, I'll be forced to wring your American cockiness from you using heavy rollers. Your *respectful* request is denied."

Yang stopped speaking and simply stared. Billy returned the man's challenging gaze. *This is a playground staring contest.* His musing was interrupted when Yang suddenly sat forward, placing fisted hands on his desk.

"Sergeant Ash. Although I'm sure I'll regret it, you will remain in your current position. However, Sergeants Water and

Rodriguez are inferior and will be demoted to Squad Leaders. You will deliver the Form 85-Performance Related Demotion to them personally. We are expanding our forces, adding patrols, which is the only reason you're retaining your position. These opposing actions may be too much for your thick, American skull to understand. Do not fear, I'll explain during my address to our soldiers tomorrow morning. I hope I've clarified that superior leadership has taken control of the Cleveland Chapter of the Citizen Soldiers. We will improve and shake free of your nation's penchant for languor. *Now* you are dismissed. Inform Private Fulbright I wish to speak with him."

Billy hesitated. He'd prepared to be questioned about the weapons inspections or the incident at Thatcher's home. Yang, speaking with Fulbright without Billy being present, sent anxiety crashing through him.

"I said dismissed!" Yang yelled, startling Billy from his trance.

"Yes sir," Billy answered.

***

As he approached Thatcher, who was seated at his pristine workstation, the man's calm demeanor confused Billy. The room was chaotic only moments ago. He glanced around. The office now appeared immaculate. Citizen Soldiers toiled away as Bai and Fan conducted white-glove inspections. It was unsettling.

"Fulbright, Captain Yang wants you in his office, pronto. Follow me."

Thatcher sprang from his chair and fell in line behind Billy. From over his shoulder, Billy whispered, "Stick to the story. Answer his questions and shut up. Do not offer commentary."

As they reached Yang's office, Billy turned to face Thatcher. It startled Billy when the man saluted, spun towards Yang's open door, and asked permission to enter.

As the door clicked shut, Billy muttered, "Don't screw this up."

Chapter 18

3:01 p.m., January 4th, Stinger Machinery

Randy's anticipatory stare felt like a white-hot light shining on Jack as he leafed through the document his friend had given him. Separated into two sections, it held a level of detail he'd come to expect from his friend.

Willis, his copy resting in his lap, studied the document carefully. His military background taught him to focus on identifying the information's shortcomings. He hadn't been able to punch a hole in it ... yet.

Jack glanced up as Crestwater made his third pass of Jack's office. "Agent, I told you before, you're welcome to join us. I think Randy's proposal is spot on."

"Jack, I haven't a moment to spare. However, I'd like to review the document independently of your brain trust's gaggle."

"That's a good idea. I'm sure you'll be impressed with the improvements he's suggesting," Jack answered, then signed to Randy—while struggling through the new sign language he'd developed—to give Agent Crestwater a copy of the document.

With his back to Crestwater, Randy grinned, then retrieved the copy he'd prepared specifically for the agent. Crestwater snatched it from his outstretched hand and read the cover sheet:

"Propellant Improvement Proposal With Projected Ballistic Coefficients Impact."

"My, my, this should prove to be a stimulating read," he said while retreating to his office.

Jack heard Crestwater shut his office door and waited for his phone to ring. Fifteen seconds later, the agent's number appeared as an incoming call. "You really should join us. Randy will answer all of your questions."

"No thank you, Mister Stinger. I'm quite capable of conceptualizing this information. I simply require a nudge in its connotation. So, enlighten me, where amongst the countless pages of mathematical computations would a person find the results and financial implications?"

"Agent Crestwater, there are no cliff notes. Only formulations accompanied by brief solution justifications. Utilizing existing resources, we'd incur zero financial output for materials. Our product will, however, become much more lethal. Additionally, the proposal, if adopted, would trim thousands of dollars in production cost."

"I see," Crestwater shot back. "Then I'll require you to convene with me later to compare notes on this project's feasibility. Please prepare to defend your position."

Jack nodded and chuckled when the call ended abruptly. "Nice work," he signed to Randy. "That'll keep him busy for hours. What information did you include in his copy?"

Randy nodded and signed, "I copied about four hundred lines of load data from the Lyman's reloading handbook and added several hundred of my own. Then, for each, I used my mom's pancake recipe for mixing the powders. It's gibberish."

Jack chuckled at Randy's sleight of hand. He noticed UW had ignored the entire exchange. His eyes remained focused solely on Randy's proposal.

Jack cleared his throat to get his uncle's attention but UW's eyes continued tracking left to right as he scoured the information.

"UW, what do you think?"

"I think Crestwater is an ass and he's afraid of me," he signed. "I also think Randy nailed it. I can't find any factual flaws. The updated signing protocols will prove challenging at first but seem familiar enough to adopt quickly. I'll send them to the teams tonight. As for the drone, bring it here tomorrow. I'll take it home and test it for noise and performance. We'll transfer it to my truck before Crestwater arrives. Zero-six-hundred should work."

Jack watched Randy swell with pride. The man simply wanted to contribute and become an integral part of the team. He had reason to be proud. Having ideas accepted by UW after his first review was an experience Jack was unfamiliar with. His uncle wasn't concerned with one's feelings; success was his primary focus. Jack and Lisa spent days convincing him the projectile launcher was their best option for assaulting the IX Center. UW excelled at unearthing the smallest faults in any strategy, especially when lives were at stake.

UW startled, his cargo pocket buzzing. "Gentlemen, if you'll excuse me," he said as he rushed from the office, leaving Jack and Randy perplexed.

Their confusion only deepened when Jack noticed UW outside, walking towards his truck. Thirty seconds later, he was driving from Stinger Machinery's parking lot.

"Jack, is today a holiday I'm unaware of? Or has your Neanderthal of an uncle finally resigned?" Crestwater, suddenly standing at Jack's office threshold, asked.

Caught off guard, Jack searched for a response, then said, "UW started feeling ill. Came on suddenly. He said something about a bad tuna sandwich. Judging by the noise his stomach was making, he may not make it home … if you know what I mean."

Crestwater's face wrinkled in disgust. "Yes, I understand the message you're conveying. I suggest you strive to be less vulgar. This is a place of business, not your swill-soaked corner bar. We strive for professionalism inside these walls. Dock his pay for the time he's missing. I'm also considering docking your pay if the two of you don't return to your assigned duties within the minute."

Jack's brow furrowed. Crestwater's threat didn't sit well. "Randy," he signed. "Head back to the shop. We'll finish the review tomorrow, but I think it's a winner."

"Agent, have a seat," Jack began. "We need to talk."

"I'll stand, thank you. And I agree a discussion has become necessary. Let me begin. I didn't raise concerns when you ceased submitting your conversation transcripts—indeed, they can be cumbersome—and I've developed a sliver of understanding of sign language and no longer require them. Nor did I object when you maintained your office instead of setting up a workstation in the shop to facilitate monitoring of our team. However, I draw a line at encouraging non-managerial staff to wander the path of free thought. Stinger Machinery is not a co-op or employee-owned business; we have a structure. We will adhere to said structure and stop wasting time."

"So, I'm assuming I won't be defending my position on Randy's proposal?"

"How observant, Mister Stinger. Please explain *your* decision to Randy. Now return to your toils and I expect you to cover for Willis in his absence. Good day."

"So much for trusting your team," Jack sneered to the retreating agent's back.

CHAPTER 19

3:32 P.M., JANUARY 4TH, WILLIS STINGER

Willis stared at his sat-phone. He'd been expecting the text from Major General Stein, but his gut still clenched. He glanced at Stinger Machinery's office windows and realized the call couldn't happen in the parking lot. *Think fast, Jack. Crestwater's going to shit himself when he sees me leaving.* He pushed the thought away and pulled from the lot. As he reached the first stoplight, he hit send and placed the call on speaker.

"Willis, we have thirty seconds. Listen closely. Whatever you have planned, execute it A-SAP. I have a list of names I'll send later today. Contact them. It's time to ramp up. Something is happening; something I don't have clearance for. From the amount of Chinese nationals being hired by the Pentagon as consultants, my guess is Genus already capitulated. Willis, the vise is tightening."

The call ended as abruptly as it had started. Willis moved on instinct, first sending a text to Lisa, then to Callahan.

***

Lisa read Willis' text for the third time, and it hadn't changed.

"Activate Pittsburg-St. Louis-LA. OTD. 2300-J4."

Willis using his sat-phone while at work chilled her. Something was breaking. The "One Then Dark" code proved it. Was he creating a diversion or was his overarching strategy launching?

She stuffed her questions. Willis wouldn't have risked contacting her without cause. She opened her laptop's texting program, flipped through her book of contacts, entered their numbers into the program, and typed a simple message: *CODE IS: Eternal Vigilance. ACTION IS: OTD. ACTION DATE: J4-2300, Local.*

As she awaited confirmation, her sat-phone buzzed. It was Billy.

"Now."

With a crooked grin, she texted Mathews, "Now. Text Jack when you're released from the hospital. Don't forget the rock."

"I can't stand. I'm stuck in my chair." Mathews' text erased her smile.

"Move, NOW," she replied.

Three dings pulled Lisa's attention to her laptop. "Hell yeah!" she exclaimed after reading the messages.

Her sat-phone buzzed. "On my feet, moving slow, need more time."

Lisa pulled up Billy's text and thumbed, "Need five extra."

"Done," Billy replied.

Toggling back to Mathews' text, she typed, "You have four extra. MOVE!" Shaving a minute would ensure he was in position when Billy arrived.

Refocusing on her laptop text program, Lisa typed, "Godspeed."

***

Mathews knelt on the walkway, staring at the rock. Blocked by shrubs to his left and Thatcher's house to his right, he wasn't concerned about witnesses. He heard the transport turn onto the street, pulled in a deep breath, and lowered his chest onto the fist-sized rock.

The instant his full weight rested on what now felt like a Plymouth-Rock-sized boulder, his body revolted. His brain begged for mercy as spasms rocked his arms and legs, causing a grinding noise to emit from his chest. He felt his consciousness slipping and screamed to beat back the darkness closing around him.

A hand on his back startled him. "Help me! For the love of God, whoever you are, please help me!"

"What happened? Can you stand?" Billy asked.

"I have no idea. I came outside for some air and woke up here. I must've slipped on some ice. I tried to get up … but the pain—oh, Jesus, God almighty."

"Remain still," Thatcher said. "I'll radio for medical assistance."

"I can't remain still! Something's trapped under me. I think it shattered my ribs."

Thatcher radioed Citizen Soldier HQ, requested an ambulance, and looked questioningly at Billy.

"I'll lift him. You pull whatever he's laying on free," Billy answered.

"Thatch," Mathews sputtered. "For the sake of all things holy, do not touch my body."

"I'm confident I can execute this task as prescribed by Sergeant Ash. Now, please remain still." Thatcher shifted his gaze to Billy and nodded his readiness.

Billy, one hand grasping Mathews' shoulder, the other clenching his hip, gently pulled the injured man's left side off the ground. He stopped suddenly when Mathews' guttural scream startled him. It hadn't startled Thatcher, who shoved his hand into the small gap Billy had created and pried the rock free.

***

Mathews jolted awake strapped to a gurney while gray-suited paramedics loaded him into an ambulance.

"What's happening? Where are you taking me?" he asked, groggy from pain and opiates but alert enough to panic.

"Relax, we're taking you to the hospital: Saint Vincent. You did a serious number on yourself. You were unconscious when we arrived. Be thankful you were," the paramedic to his right told him.

The memory snapped back. "Thatch, I'm going to kill you … if I live! You probably caused internal bleeding. I'm probably going to drown in my blood!" Mathews hollered, ignoring the crippling pain.

The ambulance doors slammed shut, cutting off Mathews' tirade. As it pulled away, Billy turned to face Thatcher. "Did you do that on purpose?"

"Your suspicions are unfounded. I merely followed your directions. I'm sure he'll soon feel good as new."

Billy pinched the bridge of his nose, struggling with his urge to thump the back of Thatcher's head.

"Sure, whatever you say." Billy paused, choosing his words. "Now that we have some privacy, we should discuss your meeting with Yang. Go check on your son, then meet me in your backyard."

"No need. I've placed Angus in my sister's care. She's barren and jumped at the opportunity to raise Angus as her own. It's better for all involved."

Billy's shock matched his disdain for the man standing in front of him. His indifference to giving his son away—his flesh and blood—churned Billy's stomach.

"With no childcare options, I'm unable to care for him properly," Thatcher offered, answering Billy's unspoken question. "The nuisance would prove insurmountable—untenable. I've chosen to commit fully to furthering my career as a Citizen Soldier. I have no room for familial duties if I'm to achieve my goals."

"Thatcher, I think it's best for your sake we stop talking about Angus and focus on Yang. What did he ask you about Smith's murder?"

Thatcher's head tilted, confused by his sergeant redirecting their conversation. "Certainly, Sergeant. As you wish. Captain Yang was more interested in the missing BHR agents. He was curious why we were no longer searching for them. Obviously, I couldn't answer his question regarding our future search and recovery efforts. Instead, I merely pointed out that we considered the case closed once the BHR took control."

"Why would he ask you about that? It seems like a question better suited for the command structure," Billy interrupted.

"Initially, I too was confused. After several minutes of conversation, his intent coalesced. His focus became my involvement with Billson's arrest, as well as my interaction with Agent Wolfe. It appears we're not alone in our concerns with Wolfe's tactics."

"Did he mention the attack on the IX?" Billy asked, fighting a growing sense of dread.

"He did not. An oversight of monumental proportions if you query me." Thatcher's expression suddenly resembled that of the Cheshire Cat. "However, Sergeant Ash, I experienced a moment of clarity. A recalled memory, of sorts. You see, I wasn't entirely truthful regarding the disappearance of the Bureau of Harm Reduction agents. I withheld information to protect myself and my family—a fool's errand in hindsight. I suppose that's water under the proverbial bridge."

"Get to the damn point, Thatcher," Billy spat.

After a brief pause, Thatcher restarted his tedious narrative. "My apologies. I admit I often become quite verbose. That evening, I spoke to one of the agents and heard a she-her voice. Which, I'm sure you'll agree, is baffling considering the agents were all he-him."

Billy stuffed his shock and attempted to redirect the conversation. "You withheld information regarding an active investigation? Your actions violate page forty-four, section nine of the CS rulebook. It's an infraction punishable by imprisonment. You're racking up one hell of a rap sheet, and eventually, you're going to pull some bullshit I can't protect you from."

"Sergeant," Thatcher interjected. "I'm aware of my lengthy list of transgressions—and yours, I might add. I'll beg the question: What do *you* know about these egregious events? I ask because the missing BHR agents and the attack on the IX Center both follow a shadowy trail to you. One could assume you're hiding something. So, enlighten—"

Billy's hand wrapped around Thatcher's throat before he could finish, his smug expression morphing into terror. "You ungrateful bastard. You murdered a Citizen Soldier officer because he was banging your wife. Leaving me no choice but to pull your ass out of yet another fire and this is how you repay me? By insinuating I'm a traitor? Or are you threatening me? That's it, you're threatening me. Tell you what—you go tell Yang what you know. Tell him every detail. Let's see how it works out. I'm putting you on notice, you impotent little prick. You try this shit again and I'll end you. Do I make myself clear?"

Billy shoved Thatcher as he released his viselike grip, sending him stumbling backward and nearly toppling him. He glared at Billy as air pumped through flared nostrils.

"I may do just that. I believe Captain Yang to be an honorable man. With him at our helm, we will transform into the well-oiled machine our government intended. His authoritarian ways are a welcome improvement and I look forward to aligning with him and his men."

Billy, stunned by Thatcher's proclamation, watched as the ill-informed man stormed into his home and slammed the door.

"Well, that escalated quickly," he whispered.

As he stepped into the transport, his radio crackled to life. "Sergeant Ash, this is Captain Yang. Return to headquarters ... immediately!"

He brought the radio to his mouth to reply, but realized the line was silent. Yang hadn't waited for confirmation. Billy drew his Glock 22 and performed a press check. He knew what he'd find: a .40 caliber round chambered. He nodded and cranked the engine to life.

Chapter 20

5 P.M., January 4th,
Willis Stinger's Home

UW paced the command center as he waited for Jack to arrive. He should have been home twenty minutes ago.

The message he intended to have Lisa send rested in his breast pocket. The file with Randy's updated sign language was scanned and ready for distribution. He'd resisted the urge to move forward without talking to Jack, but he was losing his patience. The message had to be received by 1800 hours Eastern.

He spun toward Lisa and removed the neatly folded paper when his sat-phone buzzed. He glanced at the screen and his brow furrowed.

"Talk to me, Billy."

"Willis, we have a situation brewing," Billy answered. An engine growling in the background told UW that Billy was on the move. "They assigned a new CO to the Cleveland CS. A Chinese national! Name's Yang. He's trouble."

Willis' blood ran cold. The information lined up with Stein's intelligence.

"After we took care of Mathews, Yang called me into a meeting. I thought I was facing court-martial. Turns out, it was a mission briefing. The CS, BHR, and BCR are going full commando later this month. The hard details were sketchy, but it sounds like they've declared war on nonessentials."

"Why would Yang court-martial you? Do we need to send you underground?" Wills asked.

"Because I'm an American. He's already demoted Water and Rodriguez. He's consolidating power. I'm not going dark, not a chance, but I'm living on borrowed time. So, we have to move. We need those essential passes." Billy paused, gathering his thoughts. "Willis, they told us to prepare our soldiers for door-to-door combat. Not inspections or questioning—combat."

Willis remained quiet, sorting through the information and its ramifications. "Okay. You'll remain in place for now. Have a go-bag within reach at all times. I'm sending you coordinates to a fallback location. When I say go ... you go. I'll text you in twenty. Be available. Anything else?"

"Negative," Billy replied, then abruptly ended the call.

Willis handed the message to Lisa. "Send it to every unit. We're activating all of them. Attach the sign language file. Call out confirmations as they're received."

"UW, you need to watch this," Lisa interrupted while pointing at the monitor assigned to the southwest camera. "I've been reviewing the footage from between zero-two-hundred and zero-two-thirty. I think I found something."

The screen displayed an image of the Pilgrim Church, specifically its bell tower.

"What am I supposed to see?" UW asked, a slight edge to his voice.

"Watch the arch of the bell tower," Lisa answered as she clicked play.

The video, grainy and dark, rolled on for several uneventful minutes.

"Lisa, get to the point."

"There," she yelled, ignoring UW's sharp tone.

"Replay it," UW ordered, curiosity piqued.

After watching it a fourth time, he was certain he'd seen a muzzle flash. UW glanced at the timestamp frozen on the screen: 0207.

"That's our shooter," UW said, tapping the bell tower image on the monitor. "We *must* find whoever made that shot. Rough math, we're looking at a thousand yards in the dark. Adjust our southwest camera. I want that tower under twenty-four-hour surveillance."

Lisa responded by typing in a series of commands that adjusted the camera angle, placing the church at its center.

"UW, I need some help down here. I can't watch these monitors twenty-four hours a day. I'll eventually miss something."

"I agree, and you'll have some after Mathews gets released from the hospital."

"Not following, UW," Lisa said, her brow furrowed.

"He'll soon be reported missing. I'll explain when Jack gets home. For now, send that message. We're short on time."

UW fell silent as Jack's SUV appeared on the monitor behind Lisa's right shoulder. In the distance, he noticed a column of Bureau of Harm Reduction vehicles turning onto West 14th and out of their neighborhood.

"It's about time."

Lisa stopped typing and glanced at the screen. "The BHR finally leaving or Jack finally arriving?"

"Both," UW answered as he waited for Jack to join them. "Send the message. We've got a lot to talk about."

***

Eighteen minutes later, Lisa called out the last of the "message received" confirmations, prompting UW to send his text to Billy and Armin.

His sat-phone was ringing seconds later. First Billy, then Armin joined the call.

"Armin, I'm going to text you the coordinates of a fallback location after this call. Are you mobile?"

"Negative, my leg's a mess. The pins don't come out for another six weeks. Then I'm in a boot for a month."

"What if you *have* to be mobile? Can your family help you?" UW's emotionless words put everyone on edge.

"Yes, but it's a slow and painful process." Armin paused, his anxiety building. "What's going on, Willis?"

"It's not clear, but my gut tells me we'll be forced to relocate. Billy confirmed intel I received earlier surrounding Chinese nationals infiltrating our government. Things are going sideways and we're easy targets if they launch a full-scale offensive. I intend to change that."

"Change it how?" Jack interjected.

"When I say go, we go. We're not quitting the fight," UW answered, "but they may force us to change our strategy."

The group fell silent, each weighing UW's statement and the potential impact on their lives.

UW broke the silence. "Tonight, acting on my orders, fifty-seven units across the country will strike CS and BHR agents where they sleep. I'll be receiving a list of vetted operators who, I assume, are battle-tested. Mathews remains the only one in this group with nonessential status. He doesn't know it yet, but in the next seventy-two hours, he'll be reported missing."

Lisa shifted uncomfortably because of her inability to infiltrate the BHR's system deep enough to access and then produce essential passes. In addition, she was uneasy with Mathews disappearing. She understood what UW was planning and she didn't want a roommate.

"I'll brief Randy tomorrow morning. Tonight, each of you will gather necessities and stand ready. The future is uncertain, but I'm not. We will adapt and overcome."

Willis disconnected the call and met Jack and Lisa's determined stares before a crooked smile creased his features. "Jack, we should go upstairs. We don't want to miss Mathews' text. I'm sure Lisa is looking forward to helping her roommate get settled."

Lisa appeared to deflate as her chin dropped to her chest. "Son of a bitch," she whispered.

CHAPTER 21

5:55 P.M., JANUARY 4TH,
GOVERNOR'S OFFICE, COLUMBUS, OHIO

"What I think, Alicia, is that this is bullshit. It's ludicrous for every governor in the United States to be herded onto a plane, shuttled to DC, and then stuffed into the South Court Auditorium—especially after the Capitol Building massacre and seven governors were assassinated. Haven't they been paying attention?"

Montana Governor Alicia Sloan waited for a moment, ensuring Ohio Governor Felix Dunbar had indeed concluded his rant. She'd made the mistake of interrupting him three minutes ago and he'd been blustering on ever since.

"Don't attend. Nothing in Genus' email said it's mandatory. I'll brief you when I get back."

"Did you read the entire email, Alicia? Specifically in paragraph four where Genus ties attendance to her federal emergency funding package? How'd she put it …." The line fell silent as Felix scanned the email, searching for the veiled threat. "Here it is. And I quote: *Due to safety concerns, you are required to complete Form 85EFA-Emergency Funding Application during the Conference of Governors on January 20th. This meeting represents your single opportunity to complete and submit the 85EFA as required by federal law. Failure to submit Form 85EFA will result in emergency funds being withheld from your state."*

"Felix, I was joking. I read the email and recognize the inference. If Ohio can survive without the funding, don't go. But for the love of God, stop whining. They've destroyed the economy and the new tax code ensures they'll be collecting ninety percent of every dollar the states collect. They've created a single federal bucket. They've got us by the shorthairs, Felix. So, can Ohio survive without federal funding?"

"We need to fight," Felix shouted. "Drag their asses into court and force them to listen! This insanity must stop! Where in the Constitution was the federal government granted these powers? I'll answer: They weren't. Hell, Alicia, I can't look out my office window without seeing one of those gray-suited bastards lurking about. They're like cockroaches! Every day there're hundreds more. We've been reopening for weeks now and haven't seen a dime in tax revenue. Genus has never sought a consult. Our security services have vanished. They've nationalized every single first responder force in the country. So, tell me why Genus is suddenly interested in what we think?"

"Felix, calm down. For heaven's sake, you're going to have a stroke if you don't relax," Alicia interrupted. "If you bring up suing the administration one more time, I'm going to fly to Ohio and throat-punch you. Does Ohio still have a court system? Genus dismantled the entirety of our nation's judiciary branch."

"What's your point?" Felix blurted out.

"Stop interrupting me!" Alicia said firmly. "My point is, we're irrelevant. We've been demoted to lackeys tending to our state's budgets and there's nothing you or I can do about it."

Felix's stomach twisted. Alicia's words held far more truth than he was prepared to hear. Neither spoke for a long time, both contemplating their way forward.

"Alicia," Felix said, breaking the silence. "I'll meet you at the bar closest to our gate."

"Still hate to fly?"

"I do," Felix said wryly. "So, I'll be drunk when I arrive and shit-faced by the time we're wheels up."

"I'd say alcohol's all we have left, my friend."

Chapter 22

11:57 p.m., January 4th, Willis Stinger's Home

Willis ignored Mathews and Lisa. They'd been glaring at him since he began calling the main points of contact for each of the fifty-seven units he'd activated earlier. They'd only lost one man. He'd expected worse. His casualty projections landed at fourteen percent. However, six of the westernmost units were yet to launch.

UW understood that with each successful mission, the next grew more perilous. As word of their attacks spread, CS Command would undoubtedly place their soldiers on high alert. He resisted the urge to suspend the West Coast, opting instead to allow the boots on the ground in those areas to determine the risk.

He had one last call to make before allowing the unhappy roommates to organize their living quarters. The call connected after one ring.

"Colonel Stinger, I already gave you my SITREP. Are you getting forgetful as your tooth grows longer?"

"Killian Callahan, you still drink that Irish swill you call beer?"

"Uncalled for, Willis. Completely uncalled for."

"I have a list of names," Willis said, taking a serious tone. "They're supposed to be vetted, but I want to make sure. I'm going to have Lisa send it to you. Lejeune grunts feature heavily. Ink-stick names you recognize and trust, then get it back to her."

"Send it, I'll have it back A-SAP. But I have to ask: Are you worried about your source, Willis? He's been dead-nuts with intel so far."

"These boys and girls are still active duty and that concerns me."

"Got it," Callahan said. "Willis, Eden's thugs didn't catch all of us. I know at least a hundred hard-noses that were smart enough to keep their politics quiet. They were investigated but remained on active duty. I've wanted to reach out to them. They have access to a shitload of weapons, not to mention valuable intel. I was planning on bringing it up on our next conference call. Let's see where their heads are. I believe the risk is justified. I'll take point. If it goes sideways, I go down alone."

"Cross-reference our list with the grunts you have in mind. If you find them on the list, we'll contact them. If not, we revisit."

"Yes, sir."

"One last thing, Callahan. We're looking at a Permanent Change of Station in the next couple of weeks. If we go dark, hold for three days, then bug out. I'm assuming you have a secure fallback. Be ready to use it. Anything else?"

"PCS?" Mathews asked as Willis ended the call. "Where? Better question, how? We're entrenched, Willis. Trying to load out all this equipment and relocate to God knows where … We might as well deliver ourselves to CS HQ and make it easier for everyone."

"Feeling better, I see," Willis said, holding Mathews' stare. "Who said we'd load out *all* of our equipment? You Army guys aren't very strategic or smart."

Mathews, sitting gingerly in a small recliner positioned in front of Lisa's workstation, held no appetite for their usual banter. He needed to sleep, heal, and not relocate while nursing a broken rib. "So we abandon everything, throw in the towel, run and hide?" he fired back.

"I didn't say that, either." Willis paused for a second. "We'll talk tomorrow morning after Jack wakes up. Until then, get some sleep."

"Mathews," Lisa said after Willis cleared earshot. "You're taking the first watch. I'm going to sleep. Wake me if anything happens. Oh, and if you keep whining like a little girl, I'm going to vote to leave you behind."

"Yeah, well, I'll second that vote," Mathews shot back. "I'll take my chances with the CS. It'll be better than dealing with the Stinger clan."

He waited for Lisa to blister him but received only a soft snore in response.

CHAPTER 23

JANUARY 5TH,
WILLIS STINGER'S HOME

Jack let the coffee's aroma wash over him as he stood on the porch, the brisk morning air rousing his groggy senses. The yard, bathed in the hazy glow filtering from the streetlights and covered in snow, reminded him of his childhood. His dad would wake him just before dawn. They'd be wrapped in snow gear and headed for the sledding hills of Big Met in the Rocky River Metro Parks by first light.

"You okay, Jack?" His uncle's voice ripped the memories away as he joined Jack.

"Do you have a sled?" Jack asked absently.

"Yeah, I miss him too. Your dad was a good man. He was my best friend."

They stood quietly, each lost in memories of better times.

"I'm not sure what to make of your reaction this morning. You were as poker-faced as I've ever seen you."

"I've always loved your hunting cabin, UW. I'd move today if we could. Do you know how long it's been since Lisa and I shared a bed? Hell, she hasn't been outside in months. If they force our hand, I'm all in."

A deep rumbling interrupted UW's reply. "What the—" he whispered as a Stryker Light Armored Vehicle squealed to a stop in front of Thatcher's home. The enormous machine proved a considerable upgrade from the smaller SWAT-style APCs the CS had been deploying.

UW smiled as Thatcher hustled to the rear hatch with his head on a swivel. He and Jack watched as the hatch lowered, giving them a clear view of the LAV's interior. Seven Citizen Soldiers sat along the walls, each with a full battle kit.

"We put them on their heels last night. They're worried. The CS and BHR will start rethinking their approach to ensure our safety during these troublesome times, you know."

"UW, how do we fight that?" Jack asked as he nodded in the LAV's direction.

"Right now, we don't. We fight what's inside that machine. They'll make the same mistake every army in history has made: They'll rely on their armor to force the populace into submission. Try to intimidate and overwhelm the average citizen. But without infantry support, they'll get bogged down. When that happens, those same machines will spit frightened soldiers into the street; soldiers who, moments earlier, felt invincible huddled behind armor plating. That's when they'll understand the mistake they've made."

"UW, I'm not one to question your understanding of military tactics, but they'll cut us down before we get close enough to engage."

UW placed his hand on Jack's shoulder as they watched the LAV rumble away. "Jack, we were standing twenty-five yards away for three minutes and not one of them noticed us. Thatcher took seventy-five seconds to enter. The hatch remained open for an additional sixty. They've already developed a false sense of security. They're undisciplined, poorly trained thugs. Their only tactics are fear and intimidation, and they'll learn that most humans have a limit to how far they'll be pushed before fighting back."

"I wish I shared your optimism, but we just watched most of America willfully bend a knee in the name of safety without so much as throwing a rock to defend themselves. When these monsters roll through their neighborhoods, they'll crumble."

"Some will, others won't. Never corner a frightened animal. You may kill it, but you'll pay a heavy price. We'll revisit the list of the 85LP noncompliant … stir them up. You'll see what I mean."

Jack glanced at UW. "Do you think that's a good idea? What if one of them talks or tries to slither into the government's good graces by turning us in?"

"I didn't say we'd ask them to join us, I said stir them up." UW glanced at his watch. "We should go; I need to get with Randy before Crestwater arrives. Let's ride in together and save some gas."

***

As Jack wheeled his Yukon onto West 14th, the effectiveness of UW's strategy and the tactics it called for became clear. LAVs teamed with smaller APCs darted from house to house picking up Citizen Soldiers.

The scene played the same during each stop. Nervous soldiers rushed from the safety of their homes only to wait for the LAV to lower its hatch. UW was right; they were undisciplined and made easy targets.

"What do we have here?" UW asked as they passed a LAV with a CS waiting at its closed hatch.

"A target-rich environment," Jack answered as he made eye contact with the Citizen Soldier awaiting entry into the armored beast.

"No. Three houses ahead. A cluster of people on a lawn. Eyes on the road, Jack."

Jack followed UW's gaze. "I'll be damned. Didn't Billy tell you they shut the silent protests down?"

"He did. But, as I told you: some will, others won't. Pull two driveways down and stop."

Jack didn't question UW and soon had the SUV parked and was preparing to exit.

"Relax, Jack. I want to see how the CS handles them."

Jack monitored the group in the rearview mirror while UW used the side view. As they watched, the LAV pulled from its last stop and sped towards the group. It surprised Jack when the cluster of roughly ten protesters edged closer to the street.

"What are they thinking? None of them are armed," Jack whispered.

His chest tightened as the LAV slowed. His hand gripped the door handle as he prepared to intervene. But the LAV didn't stop. Instead, the CS in the passenger seat held up a video camera.

"He's recording them."

"Time to go," UW said.

Jack slammed the gearshift into drive but resisted the urge to push the accelerator to the floor. He noticed the LAV's pace quicken until it was inches from his bumper.

"Ignore them, Jack," UW whispered. "Slow and steady. Don't give them a reason to pull us over."

Jack's grip on the steering wheel tightened as the LAV surged from behind, quickly passed, cut in front of them, and slammed on its brakes, blocking both lanes.

UW's hand moved to his pocket, preparing to retrieve his Benchmade Infidel. "Get ready. Move when I move."

Jack reached between his legs, his fingers wrapping around the handle of a ball-peen hammer jutting from his tool bag. They waited for the hatch to lower and its inhabitants to swarm when a disheveled young soldier suddenly dashed from his house, ignoring the threat Jack and his uncle posed.

The soldier reached the LAV, pounded on the hatch, stepped aside, and waited calmly. He had turned his back to Jack and UW while fidgeting with his M4's sling, oblivious to his surroundings.

"Clueless idiots. Turn around. We'll take the Shoreway," UW said as he pulled a pen and small notepad from his breast pocket. "Slow down when we pass the protesters."

Jack swung the Yukon into a U-turn and set course towards the Shoreway a few seconds later. As they approached the cluster of people, Jack eased off the gas and noticed UW scribbling something on his notepad.

"Mind telling me what's going on?"

UW, barely registering Jack's question, continued writing. "Stirring the pot."

Chapter 24

January 5th, IX Center, Cleveland, Ohio

Agent in Command Wolfe rolled over on his cot and watched his breath escape into the frigid air. His hopes of having the power restored collapsed as he tossed the heavy wool blanket aside, the glacial temperature assaulting his weary body.

"Son of a bitch! Why don't we have power?" He waited for Veronica to answer. She didn't. He glanced at the door, searching for the light around its edges that would signify his assistant was at her workstation. It was dark. He craned his neck, searching for his alarm clock. "Huh. She isn't answering because she's not here yet. Wonder what it's like to have a warm bed to sleep in?"

Wolfe pondered the question as he rushed to pull socks over his chilly feet. "Oh, wait, I do have a warm place to sleep. Except the witch I married changed the locks. I need a hotel room. This is bullshit."

Wolfe flinched when the room was suddenly doused in light.

"Good morning, Sir. I—"

"What the hell!? Ever hear of knocking?" Wolfe barked, interrupting Veronica as he scrambled to cover his half-naked body.

"Oh, I'm sorry," Veronica stuttered. "I heard your voice and thought you needed something."

"Shut the damn door. I'll be out in a minute," Wolfe said, responding to Veronica's frozen posture and shocked gaze.

***

"Sir, I don't have an update on the substation," Veronica said, her hand stealthily blocking her nose as Wolfe leaned over her shoulder, reviewing the Form 85PT-Progress Tracker. It read as it had yesterday: *Awaiting Parts.*

"Do we know more about this Bard character or characters?"

"Actually," Veronica said as she toggled screens, pulling up Adams' Friend Me page. "I believe I've uncovered something on that front. I reviewed Adam's social media and came across several posts on his Friend Me page. Two from Bard Red, one from Bard Blue. I don't have a clue what they're talking about, but it's a start. I tried to screenshot them for you but received a Bureau of Civic Responsibility restricted access message. Same thing happened when I tried linking to these Bard fellows' pages."

Wolfe leaned in, trying to get a better view of the monitor.

"Sir, I believe the showers have warm water again. Maintenance relit the pilots."

"That's nice," Wolfe responded absently.

Veronica pushed her chair away from her workstation, bumping into Wolfe as she did. "Sir, feel free to continue reviewing the information. I'm going to get a cup of coffee and a pair of gloves. It's freezing."

"Sure, great. Whatever you say," Wolfe mumbled as he commandeered Veronica's workstation and scrolled through Adam's social media.

"Also, sir, your hair is on fire," Veronica said, testing Wolfe's level of engagement.

"Got it. Start a fire to warm us up. Good thinking, Veronica. Enjoy your shower."

"He's clueless," she whispered as she left the room.

***

Veronica, coffee cup warming both hands, peeked around the corner, checking to see if Wolfe had left her workstation. He hadn't. Three days without bathing had taken its toll ... on both of them. If he was aware of his stench, he didn't appear concerned.

"Sir, if you'd like, I can pull the information up on your computer in *your* office."

Wolfe glanced up from the monitor. "Good idea. Besides, it stinks out here. You should clean up your workstation. Not the best representation of BHR values."

"Of course, sir. Oh, before I forget: The commissary received a fresh shipment of toiletries in case you're planning on sleeping here for a while longer. The new soaps are amazing."

Wolfe tilted his head, confused by Veronica's strange offering. "Um, good to know. I have everything I need except heat. Is the power situation fixed? The backup generators aren't enough. We need power—full power!"

"Sir, the news is the same as it was fifteen minutes ago. They're waiting for parts. I'll get your computer ready. You stay here and keep reviewing Adam's information. I'll come get you when I've finished."

***

Wolfe sat at his desk, face resting in the palm of his hand. He'd been on hold with the Bureau of Civic Responsibility for forty-five minutes. They were stalling, transferring him from agent to agent before placing him on this indefinite hold and his patience was unraveling.

"Agent in Command Wolfe, this is Agent Olaf. Sorry to keep you waiting. How may I assist you?"

Wolfe shot to his feet, his fortitude crumbling. "Is this a joke? I have explained the reason for my call to no less than ten of you morons," he yelled as he paced his office. He pointed, imagining Olaf standing in front of him. "If I'm not talking to the agent in charge in thirty seconds, I'm going to come down there and tear your lungs out."

"Sir, I understand your frustration. However, vulgarity is unbecoming an officer of the Bureau of Harm Reduction. I believe an apology is in order."

"Olaf, you wasted fifteen seconds. Don't press your luck, son. Get your AIC on the phone! *Now!*"

"Agent Wolfe," a voice cut in. "This is Agent in Command Williams. Please stop threatening my people."

"You'll refer to me as Agent in Command Wolfe. And I wasn't threatening your people, I was describing exactly what would happen if they kept yanking my chain. Now, since you were listening in on the call, you already know what I want. When can I expect access to Adam's Friend Me account?"

"You shouldn't. We're not authorized to grant internet surveillance access to non-BCR entities. Imagine the nightmare that would create. We've been monitoring your attempts to infiltrate the Friend Me account in question and have intervened."

"Williams," Wolfe yelled, interrupting his BCR counterpart. "You're interfering with an active investigation! An investigation into the murder of a BHR Agent. I suggest you close your rule book and cooperate."

"You are a perfect example of why the BCR is assigned to our country's more sensitive data-gathering endeavors. Now, if you'll kindly limit your blathering and allow me to continue, I'm sure you'll find the information in my possession relevant to your investigation."

Wolfe remained quiet through Williams' effectual pause. His jaw hinged open as his tolerance evaporated, only to be interrupted by Williams.

"We have identified your persons of interest. They are siblings—Wilmot and Huguette—and are awaiting your call. If you check your email, you'll find their contact information. Good day, *Agent* Wolfe."

***

Wolfe kept Wilmot on the phone until he received the file containing the Friends of Citizen Soldiers' notes. He'd listened to the self-proclaimed intellectual ramble through his threat assessment for each person they'd been observing for roughly twenty minutes. It proved to be a mind-numbing experience.

From the conversation, Wolfe determined Flume had received at least one of their notebooks. He hoped it was the notebook dated before Flume was ordered to find the missing 85 Plumbing van surveillance team.

After several minutes of hunting and pecking, he realized the documents were sorted by date. Thirty seconds later, he was poring over the missing data.

"You stupid son of a bitch, why would you do it?" Wolfe asked just above a whisper as he reviewed the notes. He now understood what Flume was trying to accomplish, and why, when he was murdered. "You always were a ladder climber."

Wolfe jotted down the target address, filled out the Form85FAR-Field Action Request, and opened his email program. He was going to ensure whoever killed his friend felt his wrath.

"I got you, you son of a bitch."

Chapter 25

January 5th, Stinger Machinery

The rest of their ride had been uneventful, both men quietly contemplating the ramifications of their next move.

As Jack turned onto Stinger Machinery's driveway, he suddenly remembered a key piece of intelligence. "UW, I still have Phyllis' notebook—the one from that group she belonged to, the Friends of Citizen Soldiers. That information shared with the people she was watching would definitely stir shit up."

UW nodded. "It sure as hell should. We'll go through it tonight—"

"This isn't good," Jack interrupted.

Willis followed Jack's gaze. "What the hell? Were we scheduled for an inspection?"

"Nope. Turn on your gov-issued phone. We're not giving them any reason to slap cuffs on us."

"Can you make out what's on the command flags posted to their fenders?"

"Not yet," Jack answered as he ignored his usual parking space and slid into one next to the closest of the three gray sedans parked in front of Stinger Machinery.

"OA? Do you recognize that insignia? The eagle looks familiar, but I can't place it."

When UW didn't answer, Jack turned to face him. He was sketching an image of the flags. "I don't recall either of them being approved emblems." He stealthily slid his notepad into the center console. "I have a bad feeling about this, Jack. The last thing we need is you getting arrested. Keep your temper in check. Clear?"

Jack nodded his understanding as he pushed open his door.

"Shit," UW whispered as Crestwater came into view in the entrance foyer. He was ghost-white. "He's never here this early. He knew this was coming … whatever this is."

Fifteen feet from the entrance, Jack nodded at Crestwater, prompting him to burst through the door.

"Your presence is required, Jack. Your uncle should report to his workstation immediately."

"Good morning to you, Agent Crestwater. What, may I ask, is the urgent situation necessitating my intervention? Has another BELD-assigned employee gone rogue?"

"I'm not at liberty to answer that or any questions. I've been tasked with ensuring your arrival in my office. Follow me and tell your uncle to go directly to his workstation. His presence is unnecessary."

Jack glanced at UW and signed, "Stay close to the shop door. If I get jammed up, I'll signal you by saying 'All-in.'"

UW nodded. "If this goes sideways," he signed, "check the wall behind your filing cabinet. You'll find a lever tucked behind the baseboard."

Ignoring Jack's confusion, UW continued to the shop as Crestwater turned towards his office. Jack's pace slowed as the mixed contingent of BHR and CS agents came into view. He counted six grim-faced men seated in Crestwater's cramped office. His chest tightened when he noticed three M4s resting on the agent's desk.

"Gentlemen," Jack said as he entered Crestwater's office. "To what do I owe the pleasure of your visit?"

All eyes fell on him, but no one spoke.

"Okay then, I'll start. I'm Jack Stinger and you've requested a meeting with me. I can't offer any more than that until someone starts talking. Who wants to go first?"

Jack glanced around the room, making eye contact with each of the government officials. None seemed eager to take control. He assumed their mistrust of one another had clamped their jaws.

"Gentlemen," Crestwater began. "You were an inquisitive group only moments ago. May I query you about your sudden lack of curiosity?"

"I'll take point," a Citizen Soldier said as he unfolded from his seat. Standing well over six feet, his Nordic features and piercing ice-colored eyes projected confidence. "Jack, I'm Special Operator Aegir Elden of the Citizen Soldier's Cleveland division."

"Pleased to meet you," Jack responded.

Aegir gave a slight nod. "We have questions regarding the weapons manufactured by Stinger Machinery," he said as he lifted one of the M4s from the desk. The rifle appeared toy-like in his large hands. "We believe them to be intentionally inferior."

"Excuse me, Aegir," Crestwater interrupted. "I was not aware of this topic, nor will I tolerate any such accusations. Stinger Machinery produced the finest weapons in our government's arsenal. Any inference to the contrary is unacceptable and borders on defamatory. I oversaw our manufacturing process and witnessed the function tests performed at your facilities. Our weapons proved superior in every way. Your Captain Smith said as much. I understand he cannot corroborate my statement, but surely he recorded his thoughts on the Form 85EPS-Equipment Performance Summary. Have you reviewed them? Furthermore, I'd been informed this visit was to initiate Stinger Machinery's inspection of faulty weapons, not an inquisition. I formally protest being misinformed."

"Captain Smith was my mentor," Aegir said, ignoring Crestwater's protest. "He spoke highly of Stinger's firearms." Aegir's tone suddenly shifted to one of suspicion. "At least, the ones he'd used."

Two realizations struck Jack simultaneously: Crestwater, for all his bluster, was petrified. His reputation was at stake. Also, Aegir was one of Smith's four protégés and he'd be intimately familiar with their firearms.

Aegir suddenly pointed the rifle toward the floor, pressed the rear takedown pin, and hinged the M4s upper from its lower receiver. He was disassembling the bolt carrier a moment later.

"This is our primary issue," he said, holding the firing pin up for inspection. "It appears to be in-spec. However, when engaged, its overall length is insufficient for primer detonation."

Jack's mouth felt as if he'd swallowed glue. "Is that one of our rifles?" he asked, injecting genuine concern into his voice.

"Your question leads me to our second concern," Aegir said, as he set the pin down. "We don't know for certain. We attempted to trace the serial number but quickly found the number issued to multiple weapons, an anomaly that occurred throughout our inspections. Can you explain why?"

"I'm not clear on why you'd ask me that question. We used the serial numbers assigned to us. Sounds like you need to contact the Bureau of Government Acquisition."

"Mister Stinger, we asked you this question because your company supplied the bulk of the Cleveland Citizen Soldiers' weapons. The serial numbers of which don't seem to line up with multiple Form 85EOS-Explanation of Shipments."

Jack turned to face the Asian man who'd interjected himself into the conversation. "I apologize, but you have me at a disadvantage, Agent ...?"

"Zi Quan, BHR Washington, D.C."

Zi's taunting tone failed to elicit the desired response from Jack, his broken English nearly impossible to understand.

"Pleased to make your acquaintance, Agent Zi. To answer your question, I remain unclear on how an obvious clerical error at the BGA implicates Stinger Machinery? However, if you'd like me to review the records they've supplied you, I'd be happy to do so. Better still," Jack said, shifting his attention to Agent Crestwater. "Let's supply them with the serial numbers and put this matter to rest."

"Unfortunately," Crestwater began, "I followed protocol and forwarded all of our records to the BGA *after* we verified them against our Form 85PR-Production Record. A Form 85MPR-Material Purchase Record, Form 85WAR-Waste Accounting Record, and Form 85UI-Unused Inventory accompanied every 85PR. I completed each with meticulous attention to detail and delivered them on time as noted by the Form 85SOR-Signature Of Recipient, which I'll cheerfully retrieve from my office upon request."

Jack watched the agents exchange glances, appearing uncertain about how to counter Crestwater's proclamation. He recognized it for what it was; they were bluffing.

His attention shifted to the window as Randy pulled into the parking lot and he moved to end the conversation. "Gentlemen, I'm a busy man. If you have no further questions, I'll excuse myself. However, before you leave—and if Agent Crestwater doesn't object—I invite you to tour our manufacturing facility. Ask questions of our team and inspect the quality Stinger Machinery represents."

"Mister Stinger," Zi growled. "Did I say our meeting had ended?"

Jack watched as Randy exited his vehicle. He hesitated for a moment, then hurried towards the entrance.

"Well, when everyone stopped talking I assumed it had ended. Is the meeting over, Agent Zi? As I said, I'm a busy man. I don't have time to waste while you chase your tail."

Zi shot to his feet and approached Jack, stopping only inches away. "If I were you, Mister Stinger, I'd watch my mouth. We," he said, motioning to the other government officials in the room, "will ensure your products receive *special* attention. It would serve you well to remain in our good graces."

Jack held his ground, his challenging stare locked on Zi. "Stinger Machinery welcomes your scrutiny. Our focus remains on supplying our government with quality products through superior manufacturing processes. I understand you may not recognize what that looks like and again offer you a tour of our facility."

Zi recoiled, his face flushing. "Oh, yes. I sometimes forget, Americans hold themselves in high regard." Zi leaned in and whispered, "I will enjoy watching you beg for—"

"Agent Zi!" interjected an Asian man Jack had not been introduced to.

It was clear the man outranked Zi, as he quickly retreated to his seat while never breaking eye contact with Jack.

"Jack, I am Agent In Command Lin. Please forgive Agent Zi. His passion for success can sometimes turn abrasive. I'm sure you can appreciate that and forgive his lack of diplomacy. We look forward to inspecting your superior facility."

Randy's appearance at the threshold of Crestwater's office quieted Lin as Jack turned to face his friend. Randy glanced at the M4s, moved to block his hands from view, and signed, "Everything okay?"

"I don't know. Did you leave your lunch box in your truck?"

Confused at first, Randy remembered the drone tucked away in his toolbox and nodded.

"What are you doing?" Zi yelled and shot to his feet while angling for a clear view of Randy.

"Agent Zi," Crestwater said, a sharp edge to his voice. "Randy is one of our hearing-impaired team members. Jack is asking him to report to his workstation."

"Deaf—he's deaf? You allow a defective person to work on sensitive equipment? Are you mad?"

Jack's head tilted as he made a show of sizing Zi up. "He passed our height requirement, so we gave him a shot."

Anticipating a bum-rush from Zi, Jack went onto the balls of his feet. Instead of being attacked, the room exploded in laughter.

Zi's eyes widened, his rage threatening to take control. He hard-stepped towards Jack, his finger pointing less than an inch from Jack's face. "You will regret your words, Mister Stinger. I guarantee you will regret your words."

"I'm not responsible for how you receive my words. But, if you'd like, I'll write them down, make it easier for you to understand. How's your reading comprehension? Hopefully better than your spoken word."

Zi's hand dropped to his sidearm.

"Zi!" AIC Lin barked followed by what sounded like a tongue thrashing in Mandarin. Lin's posture changed rapidly. He'd become as intimidating a man as Jack had ever met. Zi's angry grunt and sudden retreat confirmed this observation.

"Jack," AIC Lin began. "You have … courage, a trait I admire. However, you must learn your place in our new One America. Failing to do so will cause unnecessary hardship for you and your family. As an intelligent man, I'm sure you understand my meaning."

The office suddenly felt icy. Jack nodded his understanding. Lin's threat crystallizing, he realized he was standing in Stinger Machinery for what may be his last time.

"My apologies to you and your men. As Agent Crestwater can attest, I share Agent Zi's passion for success and I will fiercely defend our team. This has, at times, led to unprofessional behavior. I'm confident Agent Crestwater will counsel me on methods I can employ to avoid abrasive encounters in the future."

"Well said. Your humility is inspiring. A quality Agent Zi should seek to match. With this understanding, I believe we will schedule our facility tour for a more appropriate time. However, Agent Zi was truthful. Stinger Machinery will be scrutinized. Don't disappoint: We will not tolerate shoddy workmanship. Be it through manufacturing defects or treasonous actions, a price will be paid. A very steep price. Have I made myself clear?"

"I assure you, Jack understands," Crestwater blurted. "Our high degree of quality workmanship will be maintained."

"Thank you for answering a question not asked of you," Lin said flatly and without shifting his gaze from Jack. "I now understand why your team feels disobedience is acceptable." He paused, waiting for Jack's response.

"Yes sir, you've been clear."

***

Crestwater burst into Jack's office. He'd escorted the government contingent from the building and was now having the nervous breakdown Jack expected.

"Were those our rifles? Have you sabotaged our products? I want a full accounting on my desk by the end of the day and I mean *full accounting!* Include serial number application procedure, quality control measures, and the responsibility of each person associated with the manufacturing process. Furthermore—"

"You don't see it, do you?" Jack interrupted, his tone dripping with resignation. "None of that matters. They will find fault in everything we do. They just pressed the start button on their stopwatch."

"Your observation is preposterous. Our government is and always has been concerned with quality. They're merely ensuring their business entities are aligned with their goals, something we seem to have fallen short of. What, pray tell, is this imaginary stopwatch of yours counting down?"

"The end. It's counting the seconds left of my family's legacy. The end to you, me, and every person walking through our doors. What's your plan, Crestwater? Where will you hide when they come for you?"

Crestwater went ashen. "Maybe you weren't listening. They didn't threaten me. You brought this upon yourself. So full of bravado was the great Jack Stinger, he talked himself into a front-row ticket to enlightenment. I assure you, I'll not be joining you for the show. Now, get to work. I anticipate a call from my superiors early tomorrow. You will ensure I'm prepared for that call."

Jack's empty stare held onto a picture of his father standing in front of the newly opened Stinger Machinery. Its faded color and cracked edges unable to obscure the pride in his father's eyes.

"I'll have your accounting by EOD," he said absently. "I need to check on production, then I'll get started."

Crestwater hesitated, thrown by Jack's subdued response. "Jack, are you …"

"What did Lin mean when he talked about our new One America?"

"Frankly, I don't know. I found AIC Lin a diminutive yet terrifying man, and I focused solely on the topics with a direct impact on our business. Please don't distract yourself by fretting over topics on which you hold little sway. Off to your toils."

***

UW met Jack at the shop's halfway point. His nephew's demeanor chilled him.

"What's going on?" he signed as Randy joined them.

"It's over. I'd guess we have two weeks to do as much damage as possible before they take control of Stinger." Jack locked eyes with his uncle. His intensity startled UW.

"Gentlemen," Jack signed. "I hope you're ready for what comes next."

Chapter 26

January 5th,
Citizen Soldier HQ Cleveland, Ohio

Yang's first formal address to his soldiers had begun eight minutes ago. He'd paced the length of the raised platform ever since, the room pin-drop silent. His hard features conveyed his contempt with certainty. As he began his third pass, he noticed a tremor of irritation ripple through the soldiers.

"Do I bore you?" he yelled. "Have you become uncomfortable waiting for me to speak? Your culture is addicted to instant gratification. You crave stimuli. Your entitlement places the burden of engagement on those around you. If you are uneasy or *triggered* by my words, we have no use for you. A lethal soldier is patient, cunning, and unwavering. A true warrior embraces long-suffered hours. No matter the environment, the warrior waits. He crouches behind trees, buries himself in mud, endures the ant's bite as he awaits his prey. He harnesses the pain and focuses his rage on the enemy; an enemy that has caused him to leave his family, threatens his home, his fatherland. A warrior is not concerned with comfort or distracted by self-worth. He is but a vessel who finds honor in sacrificing his life for his country."

Yang went silent, then quickly pointed to three soldiers. "You, you, and you. Stand."

Billy searched the crowd for the soldiers Yang had identified. An uncomfortable second ticked by before three fresh recruits stood and the glares of their peers fell on them.

"You are pathetic," Yang screamed. "The fear in your eyes from merely my words is disgraceful, an insult to your brothers in arms!" He paused, watching the three men tremble. "You! What is your name?"

"Private Sims, sir."

"Tell me, *Private Sims*," Yang's singsong tone mocked the young man's high pitch. "Why should your squadmates trust a weak-chinned sissy such as you?"

"I, I, um ..."

"Indecision will get you killed," Yang interrupted the stammering soldier. "If you cannot articulate why your squadmates should trust you with clarity and decisiveness, how will you react on the battlefield? Sergeant Bai, remove this pathetic creature from my sight. Assign *Private Sims* to janitorial duty. Cleaning toilets used by true warriors may aid his decision-making skills."

In less than four minutes, Yang had thoroughly humiliated and demoted the soldiers he'd singled out. The psychological impact was immediately evident. The soldiers remained perfectly still, eyes focused solely on Yang, each desperate to avoid their captain's wrath.

Yang remained silent as he stalked the length of the platform, his eyes searching for signs of weakness among his soldiers.

Satisfied, he gave a stiff nod and restarted his address. "By now, you assuredly recognize my superior leadership qualities. Gone is the poor behavior bred by Captain Smith's effeminate approach to leadership. Your apathy, cowardice, and disobedience are legacy traits of which you will be cured."

Yang paused, nodded to Sergeants Bai and Fan, then spun to face the screen behind him. Bai and Fan joined him on the platform as a presentation comprised of six bullet points splashed from the projector.

Billy squinted against the glare, struggling to read the tiny writing behind Yang. When the words came into focus, he began searching the room, hoping to find another among their ranks as stunned as he. His stomach went into freefall as he witnessed the smiles on the soldiers' faces. Then, he locked onto Rodriguez, his former counterpart, appearing to share Billy's disbelief.

"Wow," Rodriguez mouthed.

"To observe your smiling faces pleases me," Yang said, pulling Billy's attention back to the tyrant's presentation. "You will begin door-to-door combat training upon your arrival at zero-five-hundred hours tomorrow. Our aggressive timeline was dictated by a surge strategy commencing within the month. We initiate public dissident identification procedures today, code-named Operation Identification. Your sergeants will distribute the tools required to complete this task and demonstrate their application. Sergeants Chen, Suen, and Flack will buttress Sergeants Bai, Fan, and Ash. Updated squad assignments will be distributed at the conclusion of this presentation."

Yang fell silent, a tactic employed to build anticipation. "Our mission objective is clear. Identify undesirables, cull them from the herd, retrain their minds and bodies, allow them to experience the rewards garnered from hard work, and encourage them to rejoin our One America or purge them from our societal ranks. The choice will be theirs."

The presentation ended and the room remained bone-chillingly silent. Yang smiled. His soldiers were learning.

"You may express your enthusiasm."

The room exploded. Soldiers stood as they applauded and cheered the words of their new captain. Billy stood, forcing a smile, and clapped vigorously until Yang raised a hand to quiet them. The room instantly fell silent.

His smile growing in intensity, Yang simply said, "Dismissed."

***

Billy scanned the newly minted roster. Now responsible for three squads, he commanded an equal number of squad leaders. One of them was Rodriguez. He glanced up as gravel crunching under boots signaled his team was assembling.

"Squad Two, stack up behind Squad One. Squad Three, report to the supply depot, collect the signs … and return in double time. Our LAVs arrive in ten."

As his soldiers scrambled to follow his orders, Billy pulled Rodriguez aside. "You going to be okay with this?"

Rodriguez nodded.

"It's important you understand I had nothing to do with your demotion. Yang made me deliver the news, sadistic little prick."

"We're good, Sergeant," Rodriguez replied as he glanced over his shoulder. "What I'm not good with is everything else," he said, scarcely above a whisper. "Did you notice anything missing from Yang's presentation?"

Billy's head tilted. Missing content wasn't what had bothered him.

"Billy, he didn't mention terrorists, gave no updates on terrorist activity, and presented no apprehension strategy. His entire focus was on nonessentials. Oh, I'm sorry, dissidents. I didn't sign up for this bullshit."

Billy, surprised he'd missed the omission by Yang and unsure of Rodriguez's motives, played dumb. "What bullshit?"

"You can drop the act, Sergeant. You haven't been on board since day one. I don't know what your angle is, but I don't see you being okay with painting a scarlet letter on the average citizen. We may as well kill them now and save them some suffering."

"What are you getting at?"

Rodriguez grinned. "C'mon, Billy. You're not a dumbass, yet you filled your squad with the absolute worst soldiers to have ever strapped on boots *and* made Fulbright your Squad Leader. Well, let's just say, I got suspicious. But, when you got the pseudo-intellectual shit assigned as liaise to the BHR, it con—"

"Sergeant Ash, Squad Three reporting," a pimply-faced CS barked, interrupting Rodriguez. "Signs have been secured. Awaiting orders, sir."

"At ease, Sonora," Billy ordered as he stepped away from Rodriguez. "Soldiers, today's mission may seem irrelevant, maybe even menial. However, it's our first step toward reclaiming this country for the righteous. We will fan out, each LAV delivering a squad to a pre-determined sector. I will provide each SL a list of addresses. Upon arrival, each squad will secure a sign in the front yard of every house identified on the aforementioned list. You will not—I repeat, *not* engage the residents in their dwellings. If they exit their dwellings, become aggressive or combative, you are to record the incident and move on. Lethal force is not authorized. Clear?"

In unison, the Citizen Soldiers enthusiastically confirmed their understanding.

As the LAVs convoyed into place and began lowering their rear hatches, Billy gave the order to board. "Sound off as you enter. SLs check your rosters. Rodriguez, you're with me."

"Sergeant Ash, I'm most definitely with you."

CHAPTER 27

JANUARY 5TH, WILLIS STINGER'S HOME

Lisa struggled to focus on the frenetic communications within the BHR email system. She'd noticed a sharp uptick since UW activated the entirety of their cells which resulted in the assassination of hundreds of BHR and CS agents thirty-six hours earlier. The emails she'd intercepted made several things clear: The government's decision-makers were anxious, heads were rolling as the blame game ramped up, and the need for an organized government counter-offensive was the dominant mindset. But, lacking specific targets, nonessentials as a whole became the government's enemy of choice.

Willis' assessment of the government's response had been correct. They were lashing out. The suggested punishment for the citizenry grew in scope and brutality with each email she reviewed. Their attempts to outdo one another by proclaiming their commitment to Genus while simultaneously tossing their counterparts under the proverbial bus demonstrated a master class in governmental self-preservation.

Her frustration grew in line with the volume of communications. She couldn't possibly track them all, and adding to the challenge was Mathews' thunderous snoring. Sleeping upright in the recliner UW had arranged also meant he'd remain crammed into her already tight workspace twenty-four hours a day, a reality she hadn't prepared for.

After an exceedingly long, multi-leveled snort from Mathews, she gripped her pen tightly, weighing the consequences of plunging it into his throat, when movement on her leftmost monitor broke her deliberation. A CS Light Armored Vehicle was slowing to a stop in front of her roommate's home.

"What are you doing?" she said, loud enough to rouse Mathews from his slumber.

"I'm sleeping. Or trying to."

"Mathews, you have a visitor," she said, pointing at the monitor. "This beast just showed up."

After he rubbed the sleep from his eyes, they watched as a squad of eight Citizen Soldiers scrambled from the hatch and formed into two-man teams. A split second later, Billy emerged. His left hand gripped what appeared to be a campaign lawn sign, which he positioned facing the hidden security camera.

"Zoom in," Mathews said, as he leaned forward to get a clearer view before shooting pain from his ribcage forced him to sit back. His eyes went wide as the sign came into focus. "You lousy bastards, you filthy miserable …." His words trailed off as a duo of Citizen Soldiers used a rubber mallet to pound a sign deep into his well-manicured lawn. The single word message, simple in its lexis, was ominous in its intention: "Nonessential." Above it, an eagle grasping a single star.

The screen fluttered, breaking Mathews' concentration.

"I took a screenshot," Lisa said. "I need to research that eagle. I've seen it before."

Billy twirled a finger above his head, causing the teams of soldiers to scatter, each carrying a dozen or more signs.

Lisa's sat-phone buzzed, stealing her attention from the Orwellian scene. She didn't recognize the number and quickly grabbed her codebook, letting the phone go unanswered. She glanced at the phone on its third ring. One more and she'd have to destroy it. She took a deep breath as it fell silent.

Leafing through the codebook, she found the number and its corresponding code script, waited three minutes, and hit send.

"The sky would be beautiful if the sun shone bright," a voice said as her call connected.

"The sun would burn your skin. Be happy for a day without sun," Lisa replied.

"I named a man without skin. Cyber Operations Officer Maximilian Oliphant. Identification Number: 97091."

"Maximilian, you're late for the game. Why?" Lisa said after checking the information in her book, ensuring it matched the name assigned to the phone.

"Call me Max. I wasn't planning on joining the team, but current events are reshaping my thinking. Is Colonel Stinger available?"

"If you weren't planning on joining the team as you say, why'd you keep the phone?" Lisa probed, uneasy with Max's answer and eagerness to speak to Willis.

"As I stated, current events are reshaping my thinking. An example would be the Citizen Soldier LAV positioned to the south of your current location."

Lisa's blood ran cold, her shocked expression panicking Mathews.

"Put it on speaker," he whispered.

Frozen by indecision, her impulse to sever the connection and destroy her phone battled against their need for an ally with technical skills.

"Location?" she pressed, fighting to control her trembling voice.

"Knowing Willis, I'm confident you have security cameras monitoring every inch of the area surrounding your location. Find the angle covering Pilgrim Church, focus on the bell tower, and wait five seconds. Advise when ready."

"Proceed," Lisa said the instant Max finished speaking.

Exactly five seconds later, three flashes of light—barely discernible in the bright afternoon sun—appeared in the tower's arch.

The tension released from Lisa's chest. "You're a hell of a shot," she said, recalling Willis' desire to locate the sniper who'd hobbled the BHR agent named Sampson.

"I can't take credit, but it was a hell of a shot. I lost a C-Note when that BHR agent crumbled." Max paused for a tick, then said, "That's when I realized how close we were to the Colonel's base of operations. Hard to miss that ugly bastard. So, tell me, what's the move-forward strategy?"

"Willis will be in contact within twenty-four hours. Prepare for his unique form of vetting. Then you and I need to talk."

"Actually … what's your name?"

"Call sign, BA-Bravo. You get my name after you talk to Willis."

"I should have known. Actually, BA, we need to talk now. You can brief Willis."

Lisa tried to object and shut the conversation down. It violated UW's protocols. But Max plowed forward and when he finished, she wished he hadn't spoken a word.

Chapter 28

January 6th,
Eisenhower Executive Office Building,
Auditorium

Woods' stare, unwavering and contemptuous, never left the monitor as Rosos' belittling rant entered its twentieth minute. She'd begun questioning her enthusiasm for Roberts' assassination.

"So, I ask again, why exactly have you been unable to subjugate this burgeoning anarchist movement? You command the entire government with every resource imaginable at your fingertips. Yet, the equivalent of children wielding sticks has claimed the lives of three hundred and sixty of our force, wounded twice that number, and crippled a government facility. A strategically invaluable facility! Simply incomprehensible!"

"Sir," Cummings began, "I—we—share your dismay. However, we feel directing your anger toward us is unmerited. I'll remind you our strategic initiative had, until recently, been managed by Roberts. We held negligible influence over its direction or implementation."

"Your argument is invalid," Zhang shouted. "You and your counterpart maintained unfettered control of your bureaus during the entirety of Roberts' rule. Your inability to defend your assets rests at your feet. We've exercised great patience with your lack of progress. Your equivalents around the globe brought their citizenry under control and have initiated their One Nation strategies, yet you bumble through and fail at every attempt. Our tolerance has worn thin. Do not test us further."

Woods sat forward. Due to his thick accent, she'd scarcely understood a word Zhang spoke, but the words that had registered pushed her to redirect the conversation. "Mister Zhang, Representative Cummings and I will redouble our efforts on matters of security. However, dwelling on the topic of fault is both unproductive and distracts us from our meeting's goal. To refocus our conversation, I'll review the outline for the implementation of our One America strategy."

"Representative Woods," Rosos interrupted. "I see your reputation for impetuous behavior is well deserved. Under normal circumstances, it would be a welcome diversion from your country's weak political will. However, today it serves as an annoyance. I assure you, my leniency for such behavior has evaporated. Remain silent as I move our meeting forward."

Unfazed, Woods met Rosos' glare but offered no additional remarks.

"Very good," Rosos said, his sneering tone causing her teeth to grind. "Our next order of business is President Genus."

Woods had forgotten Genus was present during the abrasive dialogue. Her yelp at hearing her name only served to further infuriate Woods.

"Mister Zhang and I have reassigned military command and control from the Representative branch of government, lightening the burden you've carried. Effective immediately, President Genus will assume the singular responsibility of One America's military."

"Sir," Cummings interrupted. "With all due respect, President Genus is unfit to run an ice cream stand. Placing her at the helm of the most powerful military known to man is a recipe for disaster of global proportions."

Woods nodded in agreement with Cummings' observation when Genus suddenly found her voice. "Gentlemen, I agree with Representative Cummings' assessment. I'm woefully unqualified to assume command of our military, nor am I interested. I assumed my role to be merely a figurehead, a … a placebo for the masses during troublesome times."

"Your interests are unimportant," Zhang shouted. "I advise you against placing your desires above your country's objectives. Contact Major General Stein. Direct him to begin the second round of vetting. We must ensure our military comprises only the most loyal soldiers who will act unflinchingly on our directives and embrace our ideology."

"Alois, escort President Genus to her quarters," Rosos said. "President Genus, prepare for your address to the nation and contact Major General Stein. We expect a progress report during our next meeting. Good day."

Genus' fear of Alois was obvious as she quickly stood and hurried toward the door, creating as much distance between her and the deceptively lethal senior citizen as possible. Now a permanent resident of the EEOB with no Secret Service detail assigned to her, Genus understood her survival depended on the choices she made.

Rosos paused, waiting for the President to exit the auditorium. "Ladies, ensure the imbecile is prepared for her address. I also suggest you follow up with Stein and confirm Genus has acted on our directive."

Woods' head tilted and Rosos answered her unvoiced question. "Do you truly believe we'd allow that woman to control the military with no supervision? World War is not our goal, Representative Woods. Unifying this world is. She will fail, as she has failed at every task assigned to her. However, she will become the focus of aggression should our military revolt. Her ineptitude will further solidify you and your counterpart as One America's only hope for competent leadership. Alois will conduct routine evaluations of her progress. His presence seems to cause the President great torment. It will sadden me when her usefulness expires."

Cummings fidgeted, her seat becoming uncomfortably warm. She recognized the truth in Rosos' words; she too had an expiration date.

"Excellent, sir. I look forward to watching your strategy unfold," Woods said. "Speaking of strategies, we have arraigned the Conference of Governors for the twentieth. They'll arrive in D.C. on the nineteenth. We're flying them to Newark International where they'll board Air Force One for Andrews Air Force Base. Genus' national address begins at fifteen-hundred-hours Eastern on January 20th, which we'll declare a national day of mourning and celebration of Eden. Viewing is mandatory. Communications to that effect are being distributed to the media and via text message." She paused, reviewing the notes laid out in front of her. "I believe that covers everything."

"It does not *cover* it," Zhang said. "Are the BHR, BCR, and Citizen Soldiers prepared? Are they aware of the initiative? Assuming, of course, your incompetence hasn't gotten them all killed."

Woods glared at the man as Cummings fielded the question. "On the twentieth, our forces will begin staging at thirteen-hundred hours and will be prepared to deploy by fourteen-hundred hours. By that time, they'll have been fully briefed on the true scope of our initiative. We will brief BHR, BCR, and the CS leadership on the nineteenth during a cross-bureau joint session. Until then, foot patrols have been suspended. The action is meant to calm the populace and ensure force preservation. Patrols will be conducted exclusively via armored vehicles. Field leadership has received the OA armbands and accompanying uniform insignia and will distribute after Genus' address. We have been folding the new One America iconography into public view, building recognition and curiosity. The Bureau of Equitable Labor Distribution has prepared a preliminary nonessential assignment chart, which I've forwarded for your approval." Cummings ended her disjointed statement and awaited her handler's commentary.

"And the marking of nonessentials?"

"Operation Identification is occurring as we speak, Mister Rosos."

"Excellent! We will introduce you to your Regional Assistant Leaders next week. Good day."

The monitor went blank, leaving Woods and Cummings staring mutely. "Regional Assistant Leaders?"

"Representative Cummings," Woods responded. "I believe our expiration date is nigh."

CHAPTER 29

JANUARY 7TH,
ENLIGHTENMENT CAMP ALPHA, MOJAVE DESERT

Margaux, knees hugged tight to her chest, watched the guard enter her tent. Unable to see him clearly through watery eyes, she prepared to defend herself. She refused to fall prey to the degenerate's lust.

She stood on cramping, unsteady legs, and jutted her chin toward the shadowy figure.

"You beast! How dare you return to continue my suffering. I vanquished you before, I shall best you again," she screamed as she charged her tormentor.

Her mind flashed white-hot as the butt of the guard's rifle delivered a glancing blow to her cheek. She spun to her right, fighting for balance as her world spiraled. Her legs were unexpectedly swept from beneath her as she crashed into a musty military-surplus cot, toppling her to the hard-packed earthen floor.

Her vision swam. Trying to regain focus, Margaux stared at the tent's water-stained ceiling. Resignation took hold as a sob escaped her bloodied lips. "Do what you will and be gone. But know this: I shall persevere! I shall overcome! You cannot break me!"

"Margaux? Why are you here? Are you hurt badly? What were you thinking? When did you arrive? Oh, sweetheart, I'm overjoyed to see you."

Margaux's eyes tracked the familiar voice, her vision swimming in and out of focus. A smile of bloodstained teeth greeted her friend, Lark Billson. She reached out, caressing Lark's face to ensure the moment was true.

"I've missed you so," she said, gasping through her sobs. "Assist me to my feet. I refuse to allow the guards to believe they have beaten me." Once she was able to stand, Margaux found the guard had exited. Her show of resilience went unnoticed by her assailant.

She turned to her friend and embraced her, the familiarity of her touch easing their shared anguish.

"So, enlighten me. Why are you being detained?"

"Because my husband is a coward whose sole focus is self-preservation. He's a soft-skinned, effeminate man-child who willingly sacrificed his family to avoid taking responsibility for his actions."

"I'm quite familiar with Thatcher's treachery. He's the cause of mine and Dale's incarceration."

"I know and I'm eternally remorseful. The bald-faced lies Thatcher spewed about your husband are now vividly clear. Please forgive me, I was unaware of his devious ways. Where is Dale? Have the debauched security forces separated you?"

Lark broke their embrace and sat on an empty cot. "He's currently detained in the medical tent. A doctor—Malinger, I believe—is questioning him. We're to be the subjects of a study he's conducting. He plans to group detainees from shared geographic locations to study our interactions. After a predetermined period, we'll be separated and grouped with detainees from a diverse set of geographies. Our interactions with those individuals will also be studied. His goal, from what he shared, is to study the effect of mass formation psychosis through changing environments and stimuli. Several others will join us here after their appointments. We're to be assembled in several tents, forming a community isolated from other similarly formed communities."

Lark's robotic explanation was off-putting, almost Stepfordesque as if she were excited to take part in a forced experiment and become a lab rat.

"Does it bother you we've been locked away after being loyal, faultless citizens? That after pledging our support to Eden and living true, morally correct lives, we were imprisoned sans a trial, denied due process, stripped of our dignity, and our rights as citizens?" Margaux asked, probing her friend's mental state.

Lark recoiled, then quickly settled as if receiving an unspoken command. "At first, yes. But after several days, the stresses of everyday life melted away. Now I find reward in my assigned labor."

The world ground to a halt. Margaux's thoughts went fuzzy at their edges as she searched for sanity in her friend's statement.

"Lark," she said, taking her friend's hands in hers. "Have the guards … attempted to *visit* you?"

"That only lasts a day or so," Lark answered absently as a tear traced her cheek. "They'll ignore you when the next transport arrives."

"*Lark*," Margaux hollered, shaking her friend by the shoulders. "Have you gone insane? You're acting as if this is acceptable! None of this is remotely tolerable. We don't belong here, housed with miscreants whilst being sexually brutalized by the humanity we supported so fervently. This is *not* the society we'd dreamt of only weeks ago."

Lark shook her head, eyes silently imploring Margaux to be quiet.

"You'll make it worse. Please hush," she whispered.

"I refuse to be silent—"

"Fulbright, come with me."

Margaux turned towards the profoundly accented voice. The slight man glaring at her was neither her tormenter nor the brute who'd assailed her but shared their hard features.

"I demand to know where you are taking me."

"Oh, Margaux, please stop," Lark begged quietly.

"Listen to your friend or I will force you to listen."

"You mean nothing to me. You are but a frightened insignificant man—a tin soldier lording over the subjugated, equivalent to the common patriot twirling your phallic symbols around for all to fear. Your attempts to establish your position of control in our hierarchy are unimpressive. Simply pathetic!"

The guard cut through the space between them in an instant, grasping a handful of her hair before Margaux registered he'd arrived at her side.

After being marched through the camp by her mane, scalp threatening to tear from her skull, Margaux found herself in a large white tent. She hadn't noticed how stifling the heat was until the mechanically cooled air in the makeshift exam room prickled her skin.

As her bravado faded, she sobbed quietly, wondering how she'd arrived here, where her Angus was, and what would become of her. She wiped at the tears pooling on her chin. Pulling her hand away, she found they had mixed with the crusting blood from her mouth, a wound that in her rage, she'd forgotten.

"My word, you look a mess. What on earth happened?"

She looked up, startled by the sudden intrusion into her grief. An impossibly tall man wearing a stark white lab coat held her in an empathetic gaze.

"Your hired henchmen happened! You already know this truth, so please reserve your ersatz compassion for the next weak-minded prisoner you encounter and tell me why I'm here."

The man's brow furrowed as a frown creased his face. "Very well, then. I'm Doctor Malinger. You will participate in a study of immeasurable importance," he said as he took a seat on a wheeled stool. "You see, as the battle for our country's safety rages on, we're growing deeply concerned by the resistance of a small segment of our society. Our efforts to provide for them are consistently met with what we've deemed Free Man Syndrome or Free Woman Syndrome, depending on the identified gender. We believe it to be a mental defect identified as mass formation psychosis. It's quite fascinating, but unfortunately potentially deadly for those blinded by the affliction."

"And if I refuse to cooperate?" Margaux asked, her edge dulled by the doctor's comforting approach and hypnotic oration.

"I'm afraid that's simply not an option. In the next couple of weeks, we are expecting an influx of 'guests,' as I prefer to call them. A significantly large influx. My goal is to establish sustainable protocols prior to their arrival. Doing so will facilitate a safe transition for all involved. I'm sure you understand. You strike me as a person possessing an above-average intellect, one who'll understand and appreciate my motivations and seek to advance the solution."

Margaux shook away Malinger's intoxicating tone. "You haven't answered my question. Why am I here? Seeing I have no choice but to participate, you could have easily conveyed your message via writ, public address, or your thugs. This meeting appears to serve no purpose."

The doctor flashed an easy smile, then glanced at his clipboard. "You are extremely perceptive and my assumption about your intellect appears correct. Margaux, you're scheduled to receive not only the information regarding my study but a complete medical workup. In the cramped environment in which you live, illness can spread rapidly. Plus, it appears you could use some attention to that dreadful wound to your mouth. I must apologize for that. These newly assigned guards can be a bit heavy-handed. I believe it's a cultural misunderstanding."

Margaux's eyes narrowed, her anger rekindled. "Heavy hands aren't all they're capable of. Would you care to hear a detailed account of my time alone with one of your guards? For identification purposes, he'll be the man walking gingerly whilst exhibiting a slight limp."

Malinger seemed taken aback by her bluntness and relief washed over him when his phone buzzed.

"Excuse me, I must take this," he said as he rushed from the room.

Pleased with herself for finding her voice and putting the good doctor on his heels, the minor victory rehoned her edge.

Noticing a file Malinger left behind in his haste, her curiosity piqued, she decided to find out what information it held about her. She scooped it from the metal cart next to the empty stool. Glancing to the exit, she saw the doctor through the partially drawn curtain, engaged in an animated conversation. She turned her focus to the file. A Form 85MEE-Medical Examination Evaluation was stapled to the inside cover. Behind it was a simple two-item checklist. Her stomach roiled as she read the items: "Fit, eligible for labor therapy." "Unfit, termination recommended."

Below the checklist scribbled in undisciplined cursive was a note. Its meaning felt ominous, although she didn't understand why. *Subject may be key to 20th January deadline.*

She quickly replaced the file and struggled to regain her composure. An instant later, the doctor reentered the exam room. Appearing flustered at first, he swiftly transformed into the warm and caring healer he'd projected at the beginning of their meeting; a persona she assumed he'd crafted through years of patient interactions.

Seventy-five minutes ticked by as the doctor performed what Margaux felt was an unnecessarily intrusive physical exam. Yet, he collected only one vial of blood for testing. The doctor seemed more concerned with her physical attributes than identifying if she carried any transmissible diseases. The experience confirmed her fears. He was determining whether she qualified for labor therapy or termination.

It bothered her that she struggled to resist the doctor's allure. His intellect coupled with his mastery of communication manipulated her emotions and caused her, at times, to feel idealistically attracted to him.

The snap of an exam glove pulling from his hand caused her to flinch and refocused her on the implications of his findings. Suddenly covered in a cold sweat, she awaited his assessment.

"You appear to be in excellent health, young lady. You've taken outstanding care of your body and, in equal parts, your mind. You'll be returned to your quarters in time for dinner."

Margaux breathed deeply and realized her throat was parched. She wanted to ask for water but suddenly found herself speechless.

"Before you go," Malinger said, reaching into his lab coat pocket, retrieving a red and black cloth armband emblazoned with a block white letter O. "Beginning tomorrow, you will be required to wear this at all times. You will notice other guests donning an armband with the letter A. For purposes of the study, you're forbidden to interact with those individuals. Upon its conclusion, those who've completed all its phases will be assigned an armband displaying both an O and A. This will identify you as a respected One Community Member of One America—a status to be quite proud of."

A silence fell between them, its intensity unlike anything she'd experienced.

"Miss Fulbright, have a wonderful day," Malinger said, his smile a plastic replica of authentic. "I look forward to observing you over the coming weeks."

Chapter 30

January 7th,
Enlightenment Camp Alpha, Mojave Desert

Margaux returned to her tent with the guard at her heels but thankfully keeping his hands to himself. It surprised her to find half a dozen people milling about the space which she alone had occupied until Lark's arrival this morning. Heat radiated from the additional bodies, raising the temperature in the crowded space to hellish levels.

A man glanced at her, then at the armband clutched tightly in her hand. His eyes shifted to the guard behind her. Rooted in place, he watched cautiously until the guard exited, waited a ten-count, then rushed to her side.

"I noticed your armband. Are you coming from your exam?"

Margaux regarded the man cautiously, unsure who he was or what he wanted. She ignored him and took a step towards her cot.

"Please," the man pleaded as he stepped in her path. "I'm looking for my friend. Did you notice anyone else in the tent? Maybe you heard her name. Phyllis Bandon. She left for her appointment hours ago."

Margaux held her shock in check and tried to push past the man. Opting not to tell him his friend was likely never returning.

"Please, tell me anything you saw. She's my friend and she doesn't belong here. Neither of us does."

Presenting a neutral disposition, Margaux said, "Excuse me, sir …"

"I'm Jim, Jim Bonham. I'm sorry. I know I must seem like a lunatic, but I'm worried about Phyllis. It's time for her medication. Her heart, it's … she needs her meds."

Movement to her left pulled her attention away from Bonham.

"Is there a problem?"

"No, no problem. I meant no harm. Just, please, if you recall anything, tell me right away," Bonham whispered to Margaux as he retreated to his cot.

She rewarded Dale's forceful intervention with a tight hug. "I beg your forgiveness. If I'd never introduced you to Thatcher, you'd be a free man," Margaux whispered into his shoulder. "But I'm selfishly happy to see you."

As she and Dale joined Lark on her cot, Margaux noticed a difference in him. She found comfort in the hard confidence that had replaced his historically passive nature.

"Lark told me what happened to you. I'm sorry. I failed to protect Lark that first night, but I promise it'll never happen to either of you again."

Margaux watched anger and shame battle for control of Dale's emotions. The moment passed in silence as she placed her hand on his. Knowing that revisiting her trauma would serve only to distract her from surviving, she chose to harness it and focus her rage on doing what she now understood must be done.

"Dale," she said just above a whisper while peering over her shoulder to ensure Bonham was out of earshot. "Something's not right. Set aside the fact that we've been illegally detained and focus instead on their motive."

Dale's brow furrowed. "I'm not following. Motive for what? Our incarceration?"

"Listen carefully to everything I have to say. Our lives depend on you understanding the gravity of my words."

Margaux quietly told Dale about what she'd read in her file during her time in the medical tent. When she finished, Dale glanced at Bonham, understanding the man's friend was surely dead.

"Dale, have you established a rapport with any of the guards? A loose friendship which we can exploit to gather intelligence?"

Her friend wiped sweat from his eyes. The blazing, late-afternoon sun, now blistering their tent, had pushed the temperature to unbearable levels.

"I haven't. They're forbidden to interact with us outside of assigned duties. Plus, the language barrier with the newly arrived guards seems insurmountable. Why?"

She set a determined gaze upon her friend. "Attempt to do so immediately. We're going to flee this wretched place. We must work quickly as we have merely thirteen days to devise a plan."

Chapter 31

Pre-dawn, January 8th, Tremont

The weight of his father's 1911 felt reassuring as if his father walked at his side. Jack smiled as he, Lisa, and UW emerged from a hedgerow onto Kenilworth Avenue. They took the same path they'd used to deposit Agents Wolfe and Rook's bodies into Adam's backyard.

This trip, however, would take them across Lincoln Park, forcing them to traverse the park diagonally, exposing them to prying eyes for a dangerously long time. Their route was unavoidable and dictated by the heightened focus on the homes of nonessential persons.

They'd noticed over the last thirty-six hours that the homes of nonessentials had transformed into targets. They'd become the focus of a media-driven rage against their inhabitants' status—a status determined by a government who'd deemed them unworthy to breathe the same air as a loyalist, an essential.

The vandalism started with modest, almost juvenile, acts such as random vulgarity spray-painted on the exterior of a nonessential's dwelling. Then, rapidly and predictably, escalated into shattered windows and small fires. The nonessentials who risked exiting their homes to extinguish a blazing tree or cover a broken window were beaten by the righteously indignant mobs whipped into a frenzy by their self-proclaimed moral superiority—justifying their atrocities by proclaiming they were ridding the world of the mild mental defects holding society back.

Jack's palm brushed against the 1911's grip as he looked at his uncle. "So, UW. What else are we going to discover hidden behind the walls of Stinger Machinery?"

"Your dad was a wise man. You'll see how wise soon enough." UW chuckled. Jack's excitement was that of a child on Christmas morning.

"Watch your chatter," Mathews said, his voice deafening in their helmet-mounted radios. "Lisa, I'm disappointed. You're the smart one, why haven't you shushed them? Lord knows you're good at it. Shushing, that is."

Lisa groaned. She'd jumped at the chance to leave the command center, her first time outdoors in months. Besides catching some fresh air, getting away from Mathews was her primary motivation. Yet he still wormed his way into her life.

"Mathews, please shut up. We're radio silent until we reach the church. Your fat mouth is to remain shut unless you're identifying a threat. You're over-watch, so start over-watching and don't piss around with my camera settings."

"Wow, Lisa! If I didn't know better, I'd say you don't care for your roommate," Jack said, attempting to stifle his amusement.

"She's nasty and she snores. I'm never going to heal if I don't get some rest."

"Oh, for God's sake. I should have stabbed him with the pen," Lisa grumbled while rubbing her forehead in frustration.

"Willis for Max, how copy?" UW interrupted as they reached the mid-way point of the park.

"Good copy," Max replied after a momentary silence.

"We're at the halfway mark. ETA is under five. Remember, tell your people we're only dressed like Citizen Soldiers. Make sure they know we're friendly."

"The tower already has you in sight, providing over-watch. You're green lights to our welcome mat. See you in under five."

Lisa switched her radio off and signaled Jack and UW to follow suit.

"What are you expecting?" she asked after UW and Jack turned off their radios. "Are we sure we can trust him? I mean, he held his phone for over a year before making contact."

"I've known Max a long time, mentored him through the ROTC program. I doubt he's turned. Plus, Cleveland's his home. He knows this neighborhood better than any of us. His family lived here before it became a hipster haven. We'll maintain battle-ready postures until we're certain. From the conversation we had and what he told you, his intelligence is vital. He's tapped into dozens of government networks and he's been seeing a lot of disturbing com-traffic. This is quickly coming to a head and the risk-reward equation is a positive."

Lisa fell silent, remembering her conversation with Max and how it had set her nerves ablaze. Max had drawn an image of a hellish future. The government was planning a hard-line approach to completely control the American people. A new axiom was being batted about: One America, often referred to as One America Project or simply OA. Its details were scarce, but the method they intended to employ to achieve their objective was clear: Subjugation of the populace's desire to fight.

OA: Consent of the Governed

She recalled UW's reaction when she briefed him on her and Max's initial conversation. He developed a laser focus on the One America Project information, especially when she'd used the acronym OA. He'd grabbed his notebook and leafed through its pages until he found his sketch of the flags they'd seen affixed to the government vehicles driven by the officials who'd inspected Stinger Machinery. It was as if he'd been struck by lightning.

Max had determined, at its highest levels, government seemed insulated from the flailing, knee-jerk reactions its mid-level command structure was experiencing. Their orders to regional command and control were oversimplified, merely directing them to reestablish order and maintain reestablished order resulting in a disjointed, easily confused ground force.

Max noticed a recent change that Lisa quickly determined coincided with UW's activation of their resistance forces. Hidden among the flurry of emails Lisa had attempted to review were communications from top-of-the-food-chain officials who'd begun consolidating authority and direction while exerting an iron grip on frontline personnel. After the initial government intimidation surge, ground forces were ordered to patrol solely by LAV and only exit if required to do so. They referred to it as "force preservation."

They'd begun assigning advisers and consultants while appointing a fresh wave of foreign nationals to key positions. These recent additions were highly disciplined, ruthless, former military with no emotional ties to this country. It aligned perfectly with the Mandarin language options suddenly appearing on their gov-issued devices and approved television broadcasts.

"By coming to a head, you mean a full-blown civil war cresting the horizon?" Jack asked as they reached the furthest point of the park. From this location, they'd cross West 14th, proceed to the rear of the church, and wait for Max to guide them in.

"Turn your radios on," UW said, ignoring Jack's question.

"Max for Willis, do you copy?" Max sounded panicked.

"Go for Willis."

"It's about time you answered. Heads-up, you've got a LAV approaching your six, one klick out and closing fast. Suggest you find cover until the threat has passed."

UW heard the LAV's telltale diesel an instant later and cursed himself for going offline. He spun, trying to locate a sufficient hide when they were suddenly bathed in light.

"Follow my lead. Lisa, remain behind us."

The sound of an M4's safety disengaging was her confirmation.

"UW, our tower is providing over-watch on hostiles exiting the LAV. Quick Reaction Force is standing by."

"Engage on my order," UW answered.

Willis held up his Government Security Force badge and prayed they didn't inspect it. If they did, they'd quickly discover it belonged to a missing BHR agent.

The LAV jumped the curb and accelerated, closing the gap between them in seconds. UW expected a soldier to appear through the top-hatch, presenting an easy target for Max's sniper. Instead, a voice blared from the vehicle's PA system.

"Did you boys miss the memo? No foot patrols."

"Man, am I glad to see you. Our unit's disabled on Kenilworth," UW answered, forcing urgency into his voice. "We're engaged in foot pursuit. Four hostiles hit our LAV with petrol bombs; we lost their trail by the swimming pool. Suspect them to be heading east on Starkweather. If you move now, you may be able to catch them."

A bead of sweat traced the side of UW's face as his grip tightened on his rifle. Through the spotlight's glare, it appeared the driver was engaged in a conversation with someone in the troop-hold.

"We're on it. Move your asses back to your unit. Streets are unfriendly for soldiers these days."

When the LAV disappeared from eyeshot, the trio broke into a sprint, crossing 14th, cutting through the overgrown grounds of Pilgrim Church, and heading for its rear entrance. After passing the boarded-up main entrance, UW ordered them to stop at the building's corner. Using hand signals, he ordered Lisa and Jack to fall in behind him.

When they were in place, UW sliced the corner and peered through his rifle's optics, searching for threats. His right hand twirling above his head restarted their advance. Heel to toe, they approached the small door hidden by multiple dumpsters—a tiny entryway easily missed from the street.

UW stacked Lisa behind him and sent Jack to the opposite side of the doorframe. He tapped on the door twice and received a tap in return. He moved his M4 to high ready as the door swung open and rushed in the instant Max signaled them to enter.

Max hurried the trio through the church proper, now a perfect representation of the America in which they lived. Dust-covered pews sat empty, silenced by a government intolerant of challenges to its authority. Max set a course towards the pulpit, an area usually replete with religious iconography now stood bare, stripped of its purpose.

"The government took everything?" Lisa asked as she glanced around the space.

"Every hymnal, bible, painting, and crucifix," Max answered. "There'd been talk of rebranding churches as government information and education centers but they recognized doing so wouldn't sit well with some communities. Plus, they understood it might expose their endgame and abandoned the project. Also, you can ease up on your rifles. If I was hostile, you'd be dead or under arrest."

UW answered Jack and Lisa's questioning stares with a stiff nod, prompting them to reengage their M4 safeties and reposition them to low ready.

A few quiet moments later, they descended a narrow staircase of the one-hundred-and-thirty-year-old structure. The large, windowless, dimly lit finished basement appeared to have once served as a community hall but now housed an impressive array of equipment.

"How long have you been set up?"

"About three months. After my forced discharge, they put me in government housing with several hundred other ex-military. I rounded up some techs from my old unit, and we bolted. Bobbed and weaved across the country trying to get to my family's home only to find they had assigned it to a BHR agent. The house is empty now, considered a crime scene," Max answered. "You're Lisa—or still BA? Either way, it's good to meet you."

Lisa nodded as her eyes tracked the room. Half a dozen monitors blazed through the gloom, each manned by a grim-faced soldier. "How have you stayed under the radar?"

"By monitoring their radar, so to speak. We've tapped into their e-coms and radio traffic. We go dark when they're focused on our area of operation."

"How are you keeping the lights on?" Lisa asked, fully engrossed by Max's team. "We've had to reduce consumption in other areas to compensate for our equipment. We haven't received a Form 85ECE-Energy Consumption Explanation yet, but we're expecting one any day."

"We tapped into the power lines at the pole, bypassing the meter. But when the market exploded, it severed the connection. We had to switch to a combination of solar and wind. The church already had the infrastructure in place, but it was tricky getting it up and running without drawing attention."

UW grimaced. "Sorry, that was us."

"We figured it wasn't organic, especially when Emmitt set a match to it. He gave us barely enough time to shut our systems down. Damn near forced us to evacuate."

"Sir, you need to see this," a soldier seated at the furthermost monitor interrupted. "Found more chatter about One America."

"Talk to me, Phillips."

"Sir, I pulled this from our database. It's from Representative Woods to Cummings. The language is restrained, but the message is clear. The military's second purge must be completed by OA's launch date. She's worried about Genus' ability to meet the deadline."

"How the hell are you seeing messages from Woods?"

"You must be Jack. I was beginning to think you were mute. As I said, we've tapped into their electronic communications. The quantity of chatter was overwhelming, so we built a searchable database. We've been focusing on certain keywords, but it's still a daunting task. Government windbags love to prattle on about literally anything."

"Search my name," Lisa interrupted. "Use the keywords Lisa Stinger, missing person."

"She's a ghost. Went underground after they enacted martial law," UW answered Max's quizzical stare. "Woods has a special interest in finding her."

"I'm the special interest," Jack said. "Woods and I have a history and she really doesn't care for me. Actually, she hates me. I've been living in her head rent-free for damn near two years. She'd love to evict me."

"Phillips, run a search for Lisa Stinger. Other keywords: missing person."

Lisa walked to Phillips' workstation and peered over his shoulder. Jack and UW joined her as she watched the progress bar slowly creep to the right, suddenly accelerate, and disappear as dozens of emails cascaded onto the screen.

"Open the most recent email from Woods."

Phillips scrolled for a second, then double-clicked on an email dated a day earlier. Lisa leaned over, her face nearly touching the soldier's ear, prompting him to surrender his seat to her.

Lisa's gasp focused Jack's attention on the tiny writing.

"Son of a bitch. UW, we've got a problem."

Chapter 32

January 8th,
IX Center Cleveland, Ohio

Agent in Command Wolfe deleted his response for the third time in the last hour. He'd lost count of the total number over the last twenty-four hours. Receiving an email from Representative Woods was intimidating, but after reading it, he wavered between an angry response and passive obedience.

Wolfe realized his mistake was submitting the Form 85FAR-Field Action Request—or, more likely, adding the Stingers to it. His D.C. Bureau Chief immediately forwarded the 85FAR to Woods' office. Wolfe, initially thrilled that the Eastern Regional Representative reviewed his work, got caught up in the moment. He pictured the Citation for Exemplary Service hanging on his office wall, imagined himself in Washington taking the customary handshake picture with Woods in person.

She'd killed his request within minutes of receiving it. He'd been trying to determine his response ever since. Seated at his desk, wrapped in a blanket, Wolfe glanced at his watch. The realization Veronica would arrive in ten minutes shocked him from his chair.

"I'll have her wordsmith my response," he mumbled as he dragged his pants on.

***

Veronica studied Representative Woods' email and knew she couldn't allow Wolfe to send the response he'd cobbled together.

"Sir, I'm going to read Representative Woods' email out loud. Maybe her message will … become clearer for you."

"It's plenty clear, but if it'll make you happy, knock yourself out," Wolfe shot back.

Veronica, determined to negate Wolfe's response, or at least soften it, plowed forward.

AIC Wolfe, I appreciate the effort put forth during your investigation. However, we've made clear no action at the local level is to take place until further notice.

I'm not rejecting your request simply delaying it. At the appropriate time, I will grant you the opportunity to apprehend the subjects specified in your Form 85FAR-Field Action Request. Upon successful completion of said action, you are hereby ordered to contact my office directly and without delay to arrange extradition of Lisa Stinger, Jack Stinger, and Willis Stinger to Washington, D.C. where they'll stand trial for treason and the murder of government officials.

This information is classified as TS Level One. Dissemination to unauthorized persons could cause exceptionally grave damage to our national security. Those responsible for illegal distribution of TS Level One intelligence are subject to imprisonment without trial.

I commend you for your loyalty and steadfast support of your government during these troublesome times.

Veronica felt Wolfe's glare and looked up to meet it. "I'm sure you're now clear that pushing this topic any further could prove detrimental to your career. My recommendation is to respond by simply acknowledging her email and advising her you will stand down."

It surprised Wolfe that after Veronica read the message from Woods its message was crystal clear.

"Send the following response."

Veronica chewed her bottom lip, praying Wolfe had grasped the threat to his future and hers. "I'm ready, sir."

"I know," Wolfe answered, aggravation seeping into his tone. "Representative Woods. Although disappointed, the Bureau of Harm Reduction Cleveland Division will stand down until such time as you see fit to execute the 85FAR request. Respectfully, AIC Wolfe ... blah, blah, blah."

"Excellent, sir," Veronica said as the tension left her shoulders.

"I agree. It gets to the point while remaining professional. I'm getting pretty good at the politics of this job."

Veronica smiled wryly and nodded her agreement.

Chapter 33

January 8th,
Pilgrim Church, Tremont

"It had to kill her to yank her dog's leash," Jack said after reading Woods' email. "Do you have a response from Wolfe?"

"Negative, but our database won't refresh for another hour," Phillips replied.

Jack set a hard stare on his uncle. "What's our move, UW? I didn't think they'd trace Rook and Flume back to us."

"It doesn't sound like time's our friend. Max, have you been able to pinpoint the OA launch date? My gut tells me that's when Wolfe executes the 85FAR."

"Negative, Willis. As undisciplined as they've been with their communications, we haven't seen any chatter about its launch date. We've also hit several firewalls we can't breach. We're working to find a backdoor, but to date, we haven't been able to access the power grid, SOCOM, broadcast systems, or President Genus' communications. My guess is if we infiltrate Genus' communications, we get the date."

"How long until you kick open a backdoor?"

"Willis, if you snag a copy of the Green Book, we walk right in. We'll be able to unlock everything, nothing would be off-limits. But we sure as hell can't find a copy, and we're spinning our wheels. Do you have any contacts that can pilfer a copy?"

"Green leather, gold writing?" Lisa asked

Max's eyes narrowed. "That'd be the one."

"We have pictures of it. I've tried to use it a couple of times. It didn't take long to realize I was just flailing and risked drawing unwanted attention. How do I transfer it to you?"

"Lisa, what Green Book and what pictures?" Jack interrupted.

"From the 85 Plumbing van. UW found a codebook and … don't worry about it, Jack. We've gotta move. This is huge."

"She's right," Max added. "It could be a turning point. The sooner you get me those codes, the better."

"We need to work on our strategy," UW interrupted. "The government is catching up to us. We *must* prepare for their offensive. Max, what's your force strength?"

"Ten souls."

UW was quiet. Jack could feel his uncle's intensity as he worked through the situation. "Do you have a secure fallback?"

Max shook his head. "We die on this hill."

"No, we don't. We relocate. I have a plan, but some of my people won't like it."

Lisa shook her head. She knew where this was headed and agreed with UW. She didn't like it.

"Lisa's going to relocate here," UW began, ignoring Lisa's irritated shifting. "She'll be an asset to your team. The instant you determine the OA launch date, she and your tech team will relocate to my fallback. I'll supply the coordinates by sunup."

UW directed his attention to Jack. "Jack, contact Randy. Tell him to pack; he's moving in with us. We'll do it after work tomorrow. Then, contact Armin. He and his family are to be ready to relo by zero-eight-hundred today. I'll call Billy, see if he can pick them up, make it appear they've been arrested. Being in a CS Transport should enable them to avoid being stopped by BHR patrols. If not, we escort them in Smith's car."

"Whoa," Max interjected. "We have the ability to create essential passes; no need to risk them getting caught. Get me names and pictures. We'll have them an hour after."

"You have access to the badge system? I've been trying to get into that for months. How good are they?" Lisa asked.

"They're good but not bulletproof. The pass number is legit, but if they run a full scan, it'll return an error. We've been poaching numbers from active passes, so the names and pictures won't match. We tested a few of them and didn't have any issues. The soldiers seemed accustomed to getting the error message. They mostly focus on the hologram and picture."

"Jack, scratch my order on Armin's family. Tell them to prepare to relo on a moment's notice."

UW glanced around, making eye contact with each of them. Their determined stares met his. He wasn't sure if they understood the gravity of the situation, but they soon would. He worried they wouldn't accept the fact that to rebuild, you must first tear down.

"Max, we need to get every nonessential involved, and manufacture chaos. I've got a message for them. It'll be delivered by hand, so we'll need your help."

"Send the message, addresses, and timeline when you send the fallback coordinates and Green Book. We should be able to handle it."

Lisa cut into the conversation and focused her attention on Max. "Have you come across any BHR radios?"

"A few. Why?"

"Do they have tracking devices installed?"

"Nope, they're clean."

She faced UW. "I know what you're planning. I'm not going to try to stop you, but I'm going to be in your ears the entire time."

"I'm counting on it." UW smiled, then addressed Max. "Pull your team together. We need to talk."

Chapter 34

January 8th,
Lincoln Park, Tremont

"So we tear it apart? All of it?" Jack asked, breaking the silence that ensued shortly after they left Max. "It'll be chaos. People will lose their minds. The government has been wiping their chins for nearly two years, spoon-feeding them a never-ending stream of propaganda, and our plan is to rip the pacifier from their mouths. Challenge everything they've been told to believe and ask them to trust the very patriots their government warned them about. That's a monumental shift in our strategy."

"You sold me, Jack. I'm in," Mathews interjected.

"Jack, I understand how you feel," UW said as he stopped abruptly and faced his nephew. "And your observations are spot on. It *will* be chaos. Strategies flex, meeting the threat's evolution. So unless you have a better idea, I'd suggest you come to terms with our reality. Because—and Mathews can attest—totalitarianism is flawed. Soldiers have watched it unravel for millennia. Total, unchallenged power breeds contempt among the ruling class. Each level feels they have the answers. A better way. They can fix society's problems. Each raises the level of brutality inflicted on the average serf to ensure obedience. Then, in the ultimate mind-fuck, they'll convince the serf that their shortcomings are in fact the problem. Convince them it's their fault. They'll justify their cruelty exactly as they've justified the actions they've taken over the last two years—safety. The catalyst of fear will change often. They'll lurch us from one emergency to the next, each resulting in another lost freedom. The goal? Total control through forced loyalty. The answer? You, me, every single American screaming no. So, I'll answer the question you asked earlier: yes, civil war. We tear it down. At its foundation, we rip it apart."

Jack glared at UW. He knew his uncle was right, but the images of the streets red with blood, littered with the bodies of his friends and family fought for control. He'd come to terms with their current tactics and hoped they would force government to change direction, capitulate. He'd prayed the violence UW described could be avoided.

"I see you're struggling, and I'm going to ask you some questions. Tell me the last time you saw a homeless person. Or a handicapped person."

Jack's mind searched for an answer, a counter-truth to what UW's questions had implied. Instead, he stood silent.

"They're gone, Jack. Deemed untenable drags on society. The handicapped aren't welcome in a perfect society. A social order that pins your worth on your ability to serve the government has no place for a human so mentally damaged they'll scrounge for food in a dumpster. If Randy had no useful skills, he'd be gone. So, Jack, they've already declared war. We're simply answering the klaxon's call."

"Heads up, four hostiles heading north on 11th," Mathews' voice ripped through their radios.

"Armed?" UW asked as he scanned for the threat through his rifle's scope.

"Looks like baseball bats, but hold tight."

"Talk to me Mathews," UW growled into his radio.

"I've got them. One o'clock," Lisa whispered. "Heading towards Mathews' house."

Jack and UW called out their visual confirmations when the group came into focus.

"I only see bats; unable to confirm additional weapons," Mathews said.

They tracked the group to Mathews' front yard, where they stopped and glanced around.

Jack whispered, "What are you boys up to?"

His question was answered as the group bolted through Mathews' yard and up to his front porch. An instant later, the sound of breaking glass shattered the quiet.

"Engage," UW ordered. "Jack, go right. Take cover in Thatcher's bushes. Lisa, on my six."

UW and Lisa reached the edge of Mathews' property as the first of the vandals began his retreat.

"Hey, chief. Whatcha doing?" UW asked.

The man stutter-stepped at the sight of UW and Lisa, their M4s leveled in his direction. Then, recovering quickly, he continued to approach them.

"We're good here. Taking out the trash, if you know what I mean?"

"I don't know what you mean," Lisa said. "So, stop moving, tell me your name, and enlighten me."

"Hey, what the hell? Relax, we're on your side. The house belongs to a nonessential. Didn't you notice the sign? I'm sick of them. They're holding us back!"

His screeching pitch drew the attention of his friends who dropped their paint cans and, as one, moved to the edge of the porch.

"I asked three questions, son. I'll add one. Why are you out past curfew? Essential or not, you know the rules."

The man's head tilted as he moved closer, glaring at Lisa. "Since when did they let women go on patrol?"

"That, sir, was the wrong answer." Lisa twisted her rifle's stock into the man's jaw, dropping him to the hard pack.

UW engaged his laser sight and placed it on the forehead of a man moving to help his friend, stopping him cold.

"What's this ruckus about? It's after curfew for civilians, and security force foot patrols have been suspended. None of you should be here. I demand an explanation."

"Shit," Mathews whispered into their headsets. "It's Thatcher." His warning instantly followed by the creaking of Thatcher's front door. "Jack, he's approaching on your right."

Jack slowed his breathing, straining to hear Thatcher's footfalls.

"I asked a question. Answer me immediately."

Jack zeroed in on Thatcher's blustering and launched a devastating right cross that sent Thatcher to the ground in a heap. With the threat neutralized, Jack stepped from his hide, engaged his laser sight, and searched for a target.

"LAV, rolling north on 11th! Move!" Mathews yelled.

UW caught up to Jack as they rounded onto Kenilworth with Lisa on his heels. Jack heard the diesel strain under acceleration. It was mere seconds behind them.

Jack stopped at the hedgerow and covered their retreat. When he heard Lisa push through the prickly evergreens, he dived in behind her as a spotlight swept the ground he'd just been standing on.

Sweat stung Jack's eyes as the LAV crept past, then stopped a hundred feet to the east of the hedgerow. To avoid drawing attention, Jack froze in position on his stomach; he'd be stuck there until the CS patrol left.

His grip tightened on his rifle when he heard the LAV's top hatch swing open. The sound of Lisa disengaging her rifle's safety confirmed he hadn't imagined it. A rustling behind him drew his focus to UW, who'd risen to a crouched position.

With his firearm shouldered, he motioned with his support hand for Jack and Lisa to hold. An instant later, Jack heard footfalls in the street and prepared for a firefight.

He rose, perching on his elbows, and brought his rifle's scope to his eye when a voice rose above the LAV's idling engine.

"Hey, we need help. Our friend's hurt. Attacked by a CS—"

A three-round burst from the Light Armored Vehicle cut the sentence short. A startled yelp elicited another volley of gunfire.

"We've got a runner!" someone yelled as the hatch slammed shut and the LAV sped away.

***

UW stared at Jack as he stripped away his body armor. "You understand what happened, right?"

"A lot happened, UW. Which happening are you referring to?"

"They killed loyalists tonight. You saw their essential passes; you can't miss them. The soldiers who killed them sure as hell saw them. Without asking a single question, they ended their lives simply for being out after curfew. Remember what happened if you ever doubt our actions and know this: Because they were essentials, they got off easy."

Chapter 35

January 8th, Stinger Machinery

Crestwater shuffled past Jack's office door, glancing stealthily at the toiling manager.

"Agent, what's on your mind? You still worrying your pearls over the inspections?"

Crestwater tugged at his suit coat while stiffening his spine. "Mister Stinger," he began, concern tinting his voice. "Can you explain why someone in Washington D.C. would direct me to monitor your activities? At first blush, I found the request absurd. However, the petitioner was quite forceful. So much so, I rethought my position of support regarding our firearms. Suspicion leached into my psyche, and I now believe I have reason to doubt your loyalties."

"Agent, that qualifies as the single most verbose accusation you've ever leveled at me. Honestly, I don't give a rat's ass what leached into your itty-bitty psyche."

"Your abrasive response only reinforces my concern. What to do with you, Jack? Do I relegate you to the shop to perform a menial task such as janitorial duty or simply move you into my office where I can observe your labor outputs?"

Jack, realizing how freeing not caring was, laughed. "Again, I don't give a rat's ass."

"We'll determine your actual level of concern once I've decided on an appropriate course of action to deal with a man under the scrutiny of this nation's most respected leaders."

"I'm a busy man, Agent. So—with brevity at the forefront—rat's ass."

"Very well, you leave me no choice. Grab a broom. The shop area requires a thorough sweeping."

Jack rose and scooped a stack of Form 85s from his desk. "I'll deliver these to your office. They *must* be postmarked by tomorrow morning."

Crestwater bristled. "Correction: You'll complete those forms, then attend to the shop floor."

"Not according to the Bureau of Equitable Labor Distribution's handbook. It's unlawful for management to assign cross-functional duties. I'll sweep the shop after I drop these off." Jack waved the forms in Crestwater's face as he walked from his office.

Jack brushed the feet of a BELD employee as he sped around the shop. "Sorry, there's a lot of dust by your workstation."

"What the hell's happening?" asked the BELD named Svet. "Why are you sweeping? Shouldn't you be pushing paper?"

"Jack, your presence is required in my office," Crestwater yelled from the shop entrance.

"Absolutely, Mister Crestwater! Be there in a jiffy."

He glanced at his uncle as he made his way across the shop, smiled, and shrugged. UW didn't share his humor, nor did he know why Jack was sweeping the floor. They needed him to maintain his position for a few more days, and it didn't appear he had.

Crestwater, seated at his desk, looked up as Jack entered. "It strikes me as odd that you failed to probe further about the person requesting I keep the proverbial eye on you. That's uncharacteristic behavior. Your usual response, when faced with ambiguity, is to proceed with inquiries until you reach a suitable answer. This leads me to believe you're already familiar with the person and why they're worried about you."

Jack gave a slight shake of his head. "Agent, I've chosen to no longer waste my energy trying to figure out our government's motives. You see, I apply reason when I'm confronted with a challenge. My government doesn't. I've decided I will no longer suffer fools in my quest for a fulfilling life. Meaning, I simply don't care who's crawling up my ass today, tomorrow, or the next day."

"What have you done?" Crestwater demanded, pounding his desk.

Jack leaned over the agent's desk and locked him in a withering stare. "I sabotaged all of it. None of our guns will function. I've contaminated our ammunition and I'm plotting to overthrow the government."

Crestwater recoiled, his eyes wide, mouth agape as Jack glared at him. After a moment, the agent gave a soft chuckle. Then, his amusement graduated to hysterical laughter.

"Touché, Jack," Crestwater said, wiping a tear from his eye. "Point well made. Please resume your activities as manager and complete these forms."

Jack relaxed his posture and, feigning amusement, said, "I believe that's the first time I've seen you laugh. It was refreshing."

"Well, Mister Stinger, that was quite hilarious. Your ability to employ humor to expose absurdities is a gift I've long admired. However, that little ditty was next level."

"I agree. I was on fire. Let me wrap up in the shop, and then I'll finish the 85s."

"Oh, and be aware, Jack. I will indeed follow orders and evaluate your every move."

***

"You're sure it was Woods?" UW signed.

"Who else? She may have pulled Wolfe back, but that doesn't mean she's willing to let us slip through her fingers. She's watching us. It wouldn't surprise me if we're followed home."

"Should I hold off moving in with you?" Randy signed.

"No," UW signed. "We may not have this opportunity again. You'll follow us, but at a distance. If we notice anything unusual, you'll break off and we'll regroup later."

Understanding washed over the trio. They had to act.

"The 10th?" Jack signed.

UW nodded. "The 10th."

Chapter 36

January 9th,
Citizen Soldier Headquarters, Cleveland

"Why are you avoiding me?" Rodriguez whispered as he followed Billy through the rear entrance. "I told you, you can trust me. We've got to stop them."

Billy spun to face his SL, startling Rodriguez.

"I told you, I don't know what you're talking about. I'm a soldier, like you, and you need to stop talking about this shit. You'll get us both arrested. In case you haven't been paying attention, I made you my Squad Leader. I've assigned you to my LAV for every patrol since the fifth. I'm not avoiding you."

"Sergeant Ash, in my office, now!" Yang seemed to materialize behind them. The captain had a knack for stealth, projecting the illusion he was ever-present.

Billy held Rodriguez's stare as he answered Yang. "Yes, sir. Immediately, sir."

Yang began this impromptu meeting the same as he had every formal encounter. He remained quiet and stared, sizing up the focus of his disdain.

"Tell me, Sergeant Ash, did you enjoy your time working at Stinger Machinery? Maybe you even found it rewarding?"

Billy fought to hold his expression neutral. "I enjoyed my work," he answered, his mouth suddenly dry. "But not who I worked for. When the BHR seized the helm and limited my interaction with ownership, things improved." Billy stopped talking. He wanted to ask why his captain cared but had learned the pitfalls of inquiry when Yang was involved.

"During your employment, did you witness what could be deemed subpar workmanship or the utilization of inferior parts?"

"Captain, as much as I dislike Jack Stinger, I can say he manufactured quality weapons. He was a stickler for precision. I test-fired many of them and when compared to weapons supplied by other manufacturers—well, the others don't compare."

Yang leaned forward and snatched a piece of paper from his desk. "I've reviewed Smith's Prosper Not reports and am well aware of his—and to a lesser degree, your—opinions of Stinger's weapons. However, my question remains unanswered."

"Sir, may I inquire about the report you mentioned? I believe you called it the Prosper Not. I'm unfamiliar with a report by that name."

Yang grunted his contempt. "Your country has no culture. It places value on inanimate objects, chasing whatever is shiny and new while casting aside the object you'd coveted only moments before. My society places value on the entirety of our surroundings. We see meaning in the things your world overlooks."

When Yang stopped talking, Billy simply stared. He knew the silence was a trap he'd spring the moment Billy spoke.

"I'm sure my explanation escaped your poorly developed intellect. I will, as your people say, explain it to you as if you're a five-year-old. An effective method of communication for a population of dotards. We derived the title of Form 85 through the combination of the numbers eight and five, yes?" When Billy didn't respond, Yang continued. "Good, I'm happy to see you're keeping up. In my culture, the number eight sounds similar to *Fa* when spoken. This means wealth, fortune, or *prosperity*. Conversely, the number five holds various meanings but when spoken, it sounds similar to *Wu* which, in this context, means without or *not*."

Billy was startled, but not at Yang's explanation. It was his use of "we" when describing the Form 85's creation.

Yang's greasy smile signaled his amusement with Billy's realization. He steered the conversation back on topic.

"Now, answer my question: Did you witness shoddy production standards while employed by Stinger Machinery? Whether through a breakdown of managerial oversight, poor quality control, or intentional process dereliction? All seem plausible when accounting for Stinger's workforce."

"Captain, I believe I answered your question, but I will relay it in simple terms. No. I saw neither intentional nor unintentional subpar workmanship during my employment." Billy clamped his jaw shut, set his features to neutral, and waited for Yang to continue.

"Why is it, Sergeant Ash, that I'm always left with the sense you're being untruthful? If I were to ask you about the weather, I would feel compelled to walk outside to verify your report. A commanding officer must have confidence that his direct reports are trustworthy. If trust is lacking, the situation becomes untenable. I believe you continue to suffer from Free Man Syndrome."

Yang asked no question, so Billy mutely held his stare. As the awkward silence stretched, Yang shifted uncomfortably in his chair.

"What is your suggestion for improving our relationship, Sergeant?"

"Sir, I will continue to perform as I have: a dedicated member of the Citizen Soldiers." Billy spoke with drill sergeant precision.

"I doubt that will suffice. Unfortunately, we require your skills *for now*. Be aware, Sergeant. I'll be observing your every action. I cannot shake the feeling you possess more knowledge regarding our malfunctioning weapons than you claim. If I confirm my suspicions, I will bear down on your neck until it snaps. Dismissed."

***

Billy spotted Rodriguez on the calisthenics field a dozen yards away. They'd brought in large lawn equipment storage sheds to simulate resident dwellings, and Rodriguez was running his squad through breaching drills.

As the scene came into focus, Billy noticed several obvious flaws. Rodriguez stood by himself behind the portable blast shield three yards from the door. The rest of his squad was stacked up behind Thatcher along the shed's front wall.

"Forget what you've learned from TV or movies," Rodriguez barked. "We take it slow and steady. Speed kills. The 'fatal funnel' is a Hollywood myth. Stats show enemy combatants will retreat further into the dwelling. Finally, the blast shield is your fallback position only if you find explosives."

Billy glanced across the field; seven squads were practicing, all assuming the same formation as Rodriguez's soldiers.

"Thatcher, you're our breacher. Step in front of the entry point, swing the breaching ram at the door handle, and then step into the dwelling. Your actions will disorient the enemy, affording you ample time to secure your weapon in the low-ready position."

Billy held back, eager to watch the drill unfold. Rodriguez glanced at the other squad leaders, nodded, and blew a whistle sending the soldiers into motion.

Thatcher stepped forward, dragging the forty-pound breaching ram behind him. Squaring himself with the entrance, he yanked on the ram and nearly pulled himself to the ground against its weight. He recovered, grasped the ram with both hands, hefted it using his knee as leverage, and—lacking the strength to control it—limp-arm tossed the ram towards the door. The breaching ram tumbled through the air, striking the door at its base and forcing the unlocked, thin wooden door open. Thatcher waited a heartbeat, then walked calmly into the shed.

When the drill had ended, Billy moved to Rodriguez's side. "How'd you get all seven teams to go along with this disaster?"

Rodriguez flinched when Billy spoke and spun to face his sergeant. "Sir, I provided them with the updated urban combat training manual. It's extremely informative. Here, take my copy," Rodriguez said, handing Billy the manual.

Although it appeared to be an official document issued by Citizen Soldier Command, a cursory review proved otherwise. Its pages appeared riddled with multiple typefaces, fonts, and unofficial nomenclature. A hastily assembled counterfeit had fooled hundreds of soldiers and would likely get them killed.

"You better have an excellent story prepared when Yang finds this," Billy said as he leafed through the manual.

"Sir, it arrived in Captain Yang's mail this morning. Sent from Citizen Soldier Command in Washington."

Billy, head down as he read the manual, grinned. "Well, I guess they'll be held responsible for this disaster."

"They most assuredly will, sir," Rodriguez said, unable to hide his amusement.

They were quiet for a moment, then Rodriguez saluted Billy. "Sergeant, I'm looking forward to deploying with you."

Chapter 37

January 10th,
Pilgrim Church, Tremont

"Affirmative, UW. President Genus has a national address scheduled on the twentieth. She's going to declare a national day of mourning, remembrance, and celebration. All businesses will be closed, public gatherings are forbidden, and citizens must remain in their resident dwellings with no guests. Advise you abort and return."

Lisa swore if UW asked her to confirm the date again, she'd let him continue the mission at Stinger Machinery and deal with the consequences.

When UW didn't reply, she offered an alternative. "Max's team could use an assist passing out the nonessential flyers."

She waited a ten-count. Nothing. "UW, respond."

A five-count passed before she hailed him again. "UW, how copy?"

Her stomach twisted. UW, Jack, and Randy had left for Stinger Machinery ten minutes before she'd found the information in Max's database. Woods and Cummings were bickering over the content of Genus' speech, auditorium safeguards, and nonessential detainment procedures. Judging by the castigation Cummings unleashed on Woods for putting it in an unclassified email, Max concluded the twentieth was the date they'd been searching for. He speculated the launch of OA would happen during the national address, as would the execution of Wolfe's 85FAR.

In addition, the Green Book had already proven invaluable. Max estimated his team would soon have access to the government's emergency broadcast systems and a sizable amount of control over the power grid—possibly within twenty-four hours. A breakthrough she had to put in UW's hands A-SAP.

"UW, I repeat, how *copy*?!"

"Sorry, good copy. Jack was dialing Crestwater. He got a little boisterous when I slapped the phone from his hand. We're turning around. Mission aborted. ETA ten minutes."

***

"When are you planning to relocate?" Willis asked the instant he and Jack stepped foot in the basement, his eyes locked on Lisa.

"We're going in two waves," Max answered. "We can't risk being offline, especially now. First wave is en route. It'll take them two hours to arrive, twenty-four—possibly longer—to set up. Barring any issues with power, BHR patrols, and satellite connectivity, they'll be buttoned up in seventy-two hours. When they confirm, the rest of us move. They took our only vehicle, so we'll need transport. But we need to talk about something else A-SAP. Got some updated intelligence—high-level stuff. You won't believe it."

UW nodded, never taking his eyes off Lisa. She had turned her back to him the moment he entered.

"In a minute. Who determined the relocation hierarchy?"

"Me," Lisa answered, her back still to UW. "I'm not walking away from this yet. And that's the end of this conversation."

"Lisa, I think you should—"

"Jack, I said the subject is closed. Don't take UW's side. Focus on the information Max has. It's far more important than where I'm sitting."

***

"So, they've consolidated? Is that what you're telling me?"

Max nodded sharply. "They have. According to the communications we've intercepted, they've moved Genus to the Eisenhower Executive Office Building. My guess is for surveillance and access control. She's being kept on level three, one level below the BHR offices and one level above the BCR offices."

"Why?" Jack asked. "Isn't her safety top priority? Why would surveillance trump security?"

"Because she isn't running the country," UW answered, glancing up from the stack of documents he'd been reviewing. "They're using her as a pacifier; she's a familiar face to keep the public calm." He shifted his attention back to Max. "What else?"

Max moved to the laptop set up next to UW. "This should confirm your thoughts on Genus," he said as he clicked on a document named *OA Structure*. "They're adding four Regional Assistant Leaders who'll report to Woods and Cummings. All are ex-military foreign nationals that our Military Intelligence had been monitoring for years. They're the worst of the worst for human rights violations. Genus doesn't appear on the org chart."

"Where are they located?" UW asked.

"That's the head-scratcher. The EEOB, on the same floor as Genus."

Willis reclined his chair, his eyes tracking information unseen to his team. Jack recognized the look and let UW work through his process.

"I can't believe they did it. They confined the only remaining executive branch leaders in the country into one building. One beautiful, big-ass target."

"It boggles the mind," Max agreed.

"They handed us a gift. We're going to accept it. I have some calls to make. Lisa, add the date and the government's threat of detainment to the flyer. Actually, call it what it is: the coming arrests of nonessentials. Jack, assist Max's team with disbursement when they're printed. We must put them in the hands of every single nonessential A-SAP. Max, when I'm done with my calls, I'm going to ask you to round your people up for a conference call. With Armin already at the fallback, your team should be able to cut setup by a day."

Willis glanced around, making eye contact with each of them. "Max, do you have video equipment?"

Chapter 38

January 10th,
Enlightenment Camp Alpha, Mojave Desert

Corporal Martin Spangler handed the Form 85SSC-Security Shift Change document to Sergeant Phelps.

"Quiet night, Sergeant. Spotlights in D-Unit are flickering. I put a call into Maintenance. They're sending someone over later tonight."

"Is everyone displaying their armbands properly?"

"Yes, sir. We had a couple of O-Camp detainees wander into A-Camp, but Chan and Yon rounded them up with no issues. Seemed like a harmless oversight."

It was at this point during the nightly shift change when Spangler questioned why he bothered completing the 85SSC. Phelps never reviewed them, opting instead to receive a verbal recap of Spangler's notes. He'd watch as his sergeant thought through the information, his face contorting with unasked questions only to smooth out when he answered them without speaking. Tonight was different, however.

"Did they interact? You had strict orders to keep them separated. What the hell happened?"

Spangler recoiled from Phelps' prickly tone. "No, sir," he answered sharply. "Privates Chan and Yon intercepted them within seconds. Both detainees appeared sincere in their apologies and swore to never do it again. Yon applied a rifle stock to the male's foot as a warning."

"Damn it, Spangler. You jeopardized the entire study. If Malinger catches wind of this, it'll be all of our asses. Did you put it on the 85SSC?"

"Yes, sir."

Phelps ripped the report in half, then balled it into his pocket. "Fill out another one. *Do not* add the incident. Have I been clear?"

Seven minutes later, Phelps snatched the falsified 85SSC from Spangler and stormed towards the guard shack.

"Private, get your shit together," he yelled before slamming the door.

Phelps, bewildered by his sergeant's harsh reaction, glanced at his watch, realized he had twenty minutes before the mess hall closed, and rushed off.

His pace slowed as he approached the large green tent serving as Sector A's mess. Two forms seated on a bench stood as he neared, then joined him as he entered the tent. The smell of fish stew and kale-hash combined to crush his appetite as the detainees he'd entered with fell in behind him.

A cook spotted him and called out, "Spangler, why the hell do you eat in this shithole? The guard's mess always has better food. It's serving corned beef tonight."

"How many times are you going to bust my balls over this, Tommy? I told you, I can't make it across camp before they close. Tell them to open a satellite mess hall for the guards."

"Brother, I'd find a way. I cook this shit and there ain't a chance I'd eat it. Hold up, I may have some mac 'n' cheese in the back."

"Did you drop the note?" Spangler asked as the cook disappeared into the kitchen.

"Yes, but I think my foot's broken. Can you ask Tommy for ice?" Dale said.

"Is your sergeant likely to discover our plan?" Margaux asked.

"He was livid about the incident but more concerned with saving his own ass."

"Excellent," Dale interjected. "The influx remains scheduled for the twentieth?"

"As of this morning, it is. They told ninety percent of us to report to the processing center at eight p.m. The first bus is expected thirty minutes later. Camp goes on lockdown mid-day. Guard towers have orders to shoot to kill anyone outside after lockdown."

"Hey, why are you two still here?" Tommy asked as he walked from the kitchen.

"You said you might have mac 'n' cheese?"

"Young lady, this ain't for you or your friend. Let me see your meal cards."

Margaux pretended to search her pockets, then looked to Dale. "I can't seem to locate my card. Do you have both of ours in your possession?"

"Bullshit, O-Group already ate," Tommy yelled after noticing their armbands. "You're trying to get a second dinner. You know the rule: one meal per night. Get back to your tent and stop bothering the guards or I'll report you. Hell, I'll have you arrested right now. Whatcha think, Spangler? Should we lock'em in solitary?"

"Tommy, I just want to eat. If they leave now, I'll forget it happened."

Margaux and Dale quickly obliged, exiting the tent as Tommy slapped a runny heap of cheese-covered noodles onto Spangler's dinner tray.

***

Margaux and Dale broke into a jog as the curfew bell sounded in the distance. The lights-out bell would follow shortly, the violation of which would result in a reduction of daily caloric intake lasting a full week. The enormity of the camp posed a challenge they had underestimated.

Margaux tugged her pant legs up to keep from tripping on them. She had been duct-taping the hem of her ill-fitting gray coveralls to her work boots to avoid exactly this problem. Being assigned to the garment-manufacturing detail, she'd never had to test her fix under duress. She now realized she'd have to develop a permanent solution before the twentieth. The possibility of being killed because she tripped over her clothing struck her as simultaneously comical and pathetic.

As they rounded the corner—their tent now a hundred yards dead ahead—Dale suddenly fell behind. His injured foot proved too painful to maintain the pace they'd set.

"Go on, Margaux. No reason for you to be punished by these tyrants because I'm gimped."

"I'll do nothing of the sort," she countered while slowing her pace to match his. "We'll make it. Slow and steady, my friend."

Several steps later, it became apparent Dale's injury was worse than he'd let on and they risked being late for lights out.

Margaux slipped under Dale's shoulder, prompting him to shift his full weight onto her slight frame.

Attempting to distract him from their struggle, Margaux said, "Will our plan succeed? We're dependent on guards whose loyalties are, at best, suspect."

"I've known Spangler since my university days; it was a stroke of luck to find him here. I trust him to be loyal to Eden's dream. As for the guards he's recruited, his trust in them buttresses my confidence."

They were quiet for a moment, focusing on accelerating their faltering momentum.

"We possess sufficient numbers to ensure the necessary confusion to execute our ruse. Once we give the signal, chaos will ensue." Dale paused. "Margaux, people will perish. A dreadful circumstance we must accept."

The tent entrance, now mere feet away, drew her focus from Dale's words. She'd avoided contemplating the blood that would soon be spilled, choosing instead to spotlight the greater good their actions would serve.

"I know, and I do," she answered, pushing through the flaps as the lights-out bell rang in the distance.

Chapter 39

January 11th,
Conference Call, Multiple Locations

Callahan searched Willis' words, straining to hear tone fluctuation, catch nuance, *something* to signal what he was hearing was merely an option and not a hard-baked plan. It wasn't there.

"Callahan," Willis said. "Did your team finish distributing the flyers?"

"Finished last night. I'm happy to report that even I delivered one to myself. They denied my request for limited essential status."

"Very good," Willis said, ignoring Callahan's commentary on his essential status. "And your plan for the twentieth?"

"My team arrives at my house on the nineteenth; we spend the night working on load-out. We dedicate the early morning of the twentieth to preparing to engage and for evac to the coordinates you supplied. One question: Are our essential passes ready? We won't get far without them."

"You'll have the passes by morning," Max answered. "They'll arrive in the BHR inbox we set up for you. Print them, then immediately scrub your laptop. Same holds true for everyone on this call. We can't guarantee the amount of data we're planning to send won't set off alarms in Washington. I'd like to avoid some pimply-faced BHR analyst stumbling across those emails and blowing up our entire operation."

Jack had been translating the conversation for Randy. His friend's intensity was something Jack had never seen.

"When do we move on Stinger Machinery?" Randy signed.

"I'm working on that," Jack answered in voice and sign. "We jump too early and give them time to investigate, we end up at the fallback early, taking us out of the local-level fight. Too late, we risk getting hung up in the streets and miss our opportunity."

"Billy, talk to us."

"UW, it's getting hairy over here. Yang is up my ass and he's zeroing in on the M4s. The only good thing is that he's preoccupied and not paying attention to our training drills."

"What about Rodriguez? You figure him out yet?"

"Negative. He's made some attempts to gain my trust, but his patriotic turn didn't happen until after he got busted to Squad Leader. It smacks of disgruntled employee more than a patriot righting a wrong. I'm not comfortable with him, but I'll exploit him if possible."

As UW continued questioning each of the men and women on the call, Jack's thoughts wandered. He motioned to Lisa to take over translating for Randy, then stepped into the shadowy basement, skirting the glow cast by half a dozen monitors.

He needed to center himself and pull in his anger. His gut flipped with nervous energy. Jack understood why and accepted a simple fact: this feeling wouldn't go away until the first shot was fired. Waiting would be torture; he wanted it to happen now. He'd made peace with a simple truth: hundreds of people—unwilling participants—were closer to death than they realized because his family was pulling them into a fight they didn't know was coming. And he was okay with it because he now understood the price of freedom was a shared cost.

"I'm not *leaving*!" Mathews' voice shattered Jack's solitude. "I've been able to get my body armor on without help and I'm getting around much better. I'll be ready on the twentieth. Plus, you'll need every single person on this call holding a gun if you want to limit our casualties and you know it, UW. I can still pull a trigger. Plus, you'll need someone monitoring the radio traffic when this kicks off. I'm staying, period."

UW stared at his sat-phone and rubbed his temples. Lisa and Mathews' refusals to relocate to the fallback were splitting his skull.

"We'll talk tonight but I'd suggest you don't get comfortable." Willis flipped a page in his notebook, scanned it for a moment, then continued. "Bixby, Owens, Cortez, what's your status?"

"Bixby here. It's going to be messy, but we're ready at Lejeune."

"Same for Cherry Point," Owens said.

"This is Cortez. Beaufort confirms ready status."

UW nodded. "Oorah. You boys can drop from the call. Hold until you hear from me."

"Emmitt," Willis said after the Marines disconnected. "You have what you need?"

"And a bit extra. I'll be rubber-on-pavement by mid-day on the nineteenth. Make sure your people know my truck is marked Government Food Distribution and I'll be coming in hot."

UW chuckled. "Armin, did you hear that? Don't shoot the man in the government truck!"

"Roger that," Armin replied.

Jack watched his uncle, looking for signs of doubt or trepidation. The man was emotionless as he disconnected the call.

Chapter 40

January 15th,
Willis Stinger's Home

Jack, perched on the edge of a couch cushion, monitored the evening news for signs that the government had shifted strategies. He tried ignoring the Mandarin language scroll on the left of his television as best he could. There was nothing to indicate a change in the government's posture.

He grimaced as Bryn, the government-approved broadcaster currently dominating his television, introduced her favorite guest.

"Doctor Malinger, I cannot adequately express my exhilaration that you're joining me today."

"I share your enthusiasm," the doctor said through a beaming smile.

"Doctor, I understand you have an update on the possible mental condition of those citizens refusing to join our country's march to fulfill Eden's vision. Please, we're looking to you to lead us out of these dark and troublesome times. I'm even more excited by your surroundings; they tell me you're hard at work studying this deadly—yet fascinating—mental defect afflicting so many citizens of the United States." Bryn took an effectual pause, allowing the viewer to scan the doctor's environment. "Doctor, I'll turn it over to you."

"Thank you, Bryn. To confirm, I have made great strides toward both identifying and offering a solution to the mental defect encumbering our lower-functioning citizens. Through our study, we have determined this segment of society suffers from what we now know as Free Man or Free Woman Syndrome."

"Doctor," Bryn cut in. "Wouldn't Free Person Syndrome provide a more inclusive description?"

Malinger's smile faded and his eyes flared with anger at both the interruption and admonishment. "No, we've not had ample time to study the syndrome in non-binary persons. Now, if you'll allow, I'll continue. This mental defect is ingrained deeply into some, possibly at birth. However, I was fascinated by our findings that others appeared influenced into acquiring the mental defect by a phenomenon known as Mass Formation Psychosis. An individual will focus on a leader, a small data point, or trivial personal freedom and ignore the reality—or science—unfolding around them. Their blind obedience to a harmful, antiquated, and potentially deadly way of thinking is quite remarkable."

"I again find myself spellbound by your knowledge," Bryn interjected, obviously attempting to rebound from her earlier misstep. "I'm sure our viewers are as well. Now, I understand you may have a treatment or remedy for this defect. I, for one, sit on pins and needles. So, enlighten us."

"Labor Therapy," Malinger proudly exclaimed. "We will expose these unproductive individuals to positive influences through their assigned daily toils. They'll learn the meaning of societal cohesion, interact with workers outside of their destructive communal circles, and sweat away the illness they've been yoked to for decades."

"Astonishing! Simple labor is the answer," Bryn fawned. "Your brilliance is unmatched. How will you distribute your treatment?"

"I will not be involved in either its timing or enforcement. I'm preparing a draft of my findings and recommendations for review by President Genus. But I'm hopeful we'll see it launched later this year."

"We are all hopeful and eternally grateful to have you working on this challenge. It's beyond time we deal with these societal defects that continue to asphyxiate progress. Also, viewers, the good doctor will join us on January 20. Mark your calendars! You don't want to miss a moment of his wisdom."

"Thank you, Bryn. I look forward to speaking with you again. I'll leave your viewers with this: For the betterment of us all, control your soul's desire for freedom."

The statement sent Jack rushing to the command center.

***

Jack watched Randy mine Max's database for information. His fingers whizzed effortlessly across the keyboard. He realized his friend possessed a penchant for technology he'd been unaware of until this moment.

Randy pointed at the screen and glanced over his shoulder, prompting Jack to take a seat at the workstation. He had found several dozen emails Malinger was connected to.

"Let me run through these," Jack signed. "I'm unsure what I'm searching for and don't want to distract you while I meander through them."

Randy nodded and shifted his attention to the security monitors.

In no time, Jack discovered the reason why the media relentlessly cited Malinger as the foremost expert on human behavior. He merely had to read the doctor's signature block. Malinger was the chief of the Defense Advanced Research Projects Agency's Bureau of Human Science and Physiological Warfare.

"That explains a lot," Jack whispered.

After several minutes of searching, Jack noticed a pattern. Malinger wasn't the originator of any of the emails he reviewed. He only found vague responses from the man. Some email trails contained large gaps as if they'd been redacted.

"Why is your security clearance on par with Genus'?"

"Who're you talking to, Jack?" Mathews asked groggily from his recliner.

"Are you familiar with DARPA's Bureau of Human Science and Physiological Warfare?"

"DARPA, yes," Mathews answered. "That other mess of words, no. DARPA was into some creepy shit—mad scientist stuff. The Inner Armor project is a great example. Why?"

"That doctor they've been parading around on the news controls the BHSPW. And that, my friend, roils my stomach."

Mathews stretched and winced but continued extending his arms above his head.

"Feeling better?" Jack asked.

"I am. A couple weeks of bed rest did wonders. I'll be ready to rock by the twentieth."

Jack glanced at Mathews and shook his head. "You and Lisa are going to give UW a stroke, but I agree. We need as many boots as possible. You'll have to fight that battle with UW. I'm not mixing into that mess."

"Where is our fearless leader?"

"In the garage. He's on a call with his contact and didn't want us listening in," Jack said, frustration tingeing his voice.

"He knows what he's doing, Jack. Your uncle has firsthand knowledge of what happens when too many ears are listening. People get killed because they assume they understand the conversation and its details. But they're always mistaken; they only focus on what impacts them directly and ignore the rest. If they're captured, they talk. All of it jeopardizes mission integrity."

The door slid open, and UW walked into the room, interrupting them. He took in the scene and shook his head.

"How'd I end up with this motley crew?" he laughed. Then the humor left his eyes. "Jack, we need to talk."

Chapter 41

January 16th,
Joel Atkins' Home, Nonessential

Joel circled his living room for what may have been the hundredth time. Shelly didn't know; she'd stopped counting an hour ago. He hadn't looked up from that damn flyer since finding it stuck in their screen door four days earlier. Convinced he'd eventually trip over the coffee table, she'd pushed it against the wall and out of her husband's path.

"Joel, please throw it out. We don't need any trouble. Our life is hard enough because you won't—" Shelly's words trailed off.

"Won't what, Shelly?" Joel snapped. "Sign away our lives to a government that has isolated us, dictated what we eat, how we dress, and bankrupted us? They've erased our family history, removed every photo, taken our birth certificates, and placed a scarlet letter—or, more accurately, a Star of David—in our front yard. Have you seen our house, Shelly? Have you seen the words and images their brown shirts painted on our beautiful house? *Have you!?*"

Shelly flinched. Her husband's even temper had vanished. His pride trampled for what she suspected was the last time.

"Please, don't do anything foolish. This won't last forever."

Joel took a deep breath, reining in his temper. He reminded himself that his wife was trying to protect him and the few possessions they'd held onto.

"Sweetheart, it'll never go back to normal. Someplace deep inside, you know I'm right. I'll be in the basement. I need you to gather our food and take it upstairs. We're done being serfs."

"Please don't use your walkie-talkie. They're listening. They'll investigate us again. The CS warned us. If they have to come back, they'll tear out the damn walls to find it. We can't pay another fine."

"Shelly, take the food upstairs. I'll only be a few minutes. It won't be enough time for them to figure out where it's coming from. Now, go. We're moving to the second floor."

***

True to his word, Joel joined his wife on the second floor in under three minutes.

"We need to fill these up with water," he said, answering her quizzical stare.

"Why? Our water's fine. Plus, we're already nearing our allotment for the month. Filling every container we own will draw the Bureau of Resource Management's attention and bring them to our front door. Are you trying to get us arrested?"

Joel stared incredulously at his wife. He waited to see if she'd hear how insane her words sounded. Her frightened stare told him she'd never see it. She would never understand that the government had forsaken them.

"Fill them," he said. "I'm going to move the furniture from the guest room, use it to block the stairs."

Ignoring her startled gasp, he took the armful of containers to the bathroom and dropped them into the bathtub.

"What's that?" Shelly screeched. "I thought we forfeited it to the BHR?"

Joel spun to face his wife and adjusted his shirttails to cover the gun tucked in the curve of his lower back.

"It's an insurance policy, nothing more. I only have twenty-five bullets, so I won't be running around like a commando if that's what you're thinking. But I won't allow them to take anything else from us—not a single thing."

"If they find it, you'll be arrested, maybe killed."

"Damn it, Shelly. What are you missing? They're coming for us. They've marked us, now we're the enemy. I read the flyer to you. In a few days, the government will come knocking and we disappear. Do you want me to read it again?" he asked while pulling it from his pocket.

"No, I heard you the first time. I'm scared, Joel. Why would they arrest us?" she asked as tears streamed down her ruddy cheeks.

Joel fought his instinct to comfort his wife. She had to face their reality.

"When they roll down our street, we flash our lights. We watch for others to flash theirs as the flyer said. Then, we take it back."

Chapter 42

January 18th,
Willis Stinger's Home

Jack slid the last of the hard-sided multi-gun rifle cases into his Yukon's cargo hold. Collapsing the rear seats allowed him to secure an extraordinary amount of Willis' rifle collection into the now tightly packed space.

He glanced at UW as he worked on packing his truck with the rest of their supplies. Jack grinned. The impressive amount of supplies his uncle had amassed over the years was proving a challenge to fit into his truck bed while allowing the cargo tarp to cover them completely.

"Well, it's settled. We're maxed. Everything else stays," UW said as he shoved a box of medical supplies into the cab's crew section. "I'll let Randy and Mathews know—"

Randy, appearing in the doorway leading into the house, cut UW off mid-sentence.

"BHR heading in our direction," Randy signed, then disappeared from the threshold.

Jack and UW rushed to finish securing and hiding the supplies before hurrying into the house. They arrived in the living room as the BHR sedan pulled into the driveway.

"I've got eyes on two agents. One's armed," UW said as he pulled his sidearm and performed a press-check, ensuring a round was chambered.

Jack watched the agents ascend the porch, then scanned the kitchen and living room for anything incriminating. The boxes that had littered the space moments ago were nowhere to be found. He nodded, realizing Randy and Mathews must have hidden them. Where, he didn't know.

Flashing lights indicated the doorbell had been pressed. Jack moved with forced calm to answer.

"Jack Stinger, I presume? I'm Agent Howard with the Bureau of Equitable Housing. This gentleman is Agent Defranco representing the Bureau of Harm Reduction," he said, motioning over his right shoulder. "Don't let him cause you a fright. He's merely providing security. Streets have become a dangerous place for government officials."

"Your presumption is correct. I'm Jack Stinger. How have I earned the honor of a visit from the BEH?"

The bespectacled Agent Howard pushed his glasses up his nose and fixed Jack in a toothy grin but didn't reply.

"Okay, I'll ask again, a little more directly this time. Why the hell are you bothering me at dinnertime?"

"I can answer your question inside your dwelling. No reason to involve your neighbors in our conversation."

Defranco shifting to the right, creating a clear line of fire raised Jack's hackles.

"Really? You're going to shoot me because I don't want to let strangers into my dwelling, one of them carrying a weapon of murder and oppression? How do I know you're not a couple of nonessentials trying to rob me? Neither of you has offered your badges for inspection."

"Fair enough, Mister Stinger," Howard said while holding his identification lanyard up for Jack's review.

Jack made a show of reviewing it, allowing UW time to position himself in front of the basement entrance.

"You can enter, but Mister Trigger Finger remains outside. I don't want guns in my dwelling. I despise them."

"I wholly understand your hesitancy," Agent Howard said, tilting his head in empathy. "However, Agent Defranco has orders to hold fast to my side whilst in the field. I'm sure you understand."

Jack relented and stepped aside, allowing the agents to enter. Then shut and locked the door.

"Unlock the door," Defranco growled.

"I'd rather not. As Agent Howard pointed out, it's a dangerous time. Dark and troublesome. One can't exercise enough caution. If one of those terrible flag-wavers sees your car and decides to exact revenge—well, let's say I'd rather not get caught up in that ugliness."

The BHR agent pushed past Jack and fumbled with the deadbolt until he heard the snick of the bolt retracting.

"Suit yourself, but understand I'll be hiding behind you if a self-proclaimed patriot barges in shooting like a maniac."

Agent Howard and Jack sat at the table while Defranco stood guard at the door with his finger resting on his MP5's trigger.

"Jack—can I call you Jack, or do you prefer Mister Stinger? I'll just call you Jack. Tell me, were you aware of a gas leak at your previous dwelling?"

Jack's vision swam. He grappled with his panic and forced a neutral expression. "Please excuse me for my earlier rudeness. With all the tragedy that's befallen our country recently, I'd forgotten about my losses, focusing only on our grieving nation and how I could contribute to help ease our suffering. Agent Crestwater informed me you'd want to question me. I, of course, am at your disposal. Now, to answer your question, I was unaware of any defects in my former dwelling, mechanical or otherwise. I'm devastated that a place I found joy in has caused pain for others."

Agent Howard's posture stiffened, and his eyes narrowed. "How is it possible, Jack, that a vacant dwelling suddenly developed a gas leak? An interior leak to boot. Seems an unlikely event. Did you perform unauthorized repairs in the days before the catastrophe?"

"No, sir. I was a stickler for submitting my Form 85DIR-Dwelling Improvement Requests and would never attempt to complete work myself because nothing beats government workmanship. Is it possible squatters moved in?"

"For Christ's sake, he's lying," Defranco yelled, taking a step towards them. "He sabotaged the dwelling before he left. I'll cuff him. You can finish interviewing him in the car on the way to Holding."

The BHR agent allowed his MP5 to swing loose on its sling as he removed zip-cuffs from a pant leg cargo pocket. When the 9mm round slammed into Defranco's head, spraying blood in every direction, Agent Howard screamed. He dove to the floor, scrabbling to get under the table.

Jack remained seated as UW entered the kitchen with Randy and Mathews on his heels. He knew this would happen the instant the BHR agent removed the cuffs.

"Agent Howard," Jack began. "I'd like to introduce you to my uncle, Colonel Willis Stinger, USMC, retired. He'd like to know if you'd rather die on your feet instead of groveling on the floor like a little bitch?"

***

Agents Howard and Defranco, wrapped in bloody plastic tarps, rested in the corner of UW's garage. Strangely, Jack felt almost nothing. There was no remorse or grief, just numbness. He was, however, angry. A simmering rage roiled his soul. It was a rage so entrenched he was sure it wouldn't leave him until his last breath. His government had turned him into a killer, a label he'd been sure a few short years ago that he'd never wear.

In an act of defiance so minuscule calling it disobedience stoked the embers, he turned the radio on, pushing its volume over the legal limit. "Fuck you," he whispered.

"Hey, a little help? I can't get this corner secured."

Jack joined UW at the driver's side corner of the truck bed where his uncle was fighting a losing battle with the tarp's grommet. The pressure UW had exerted had deformed it and allowed the tarp's corner to come untucked. If the wind caught hold and worked it free, their cargo would be exposed. Explaining their payload to an overzealous BHR agent who may happen upon them was something they had to avoid.

"Why'd you turn the radio on?"

"Ha, I really don't know. The feeling of poking them in the eye appealed to me, I guess. Plus, it's music day. Thought it'd be nice to listen to the government-approved selection of easy listening hits. There you go," Jack said as he slid a bowline knot into place, securing the tarp. "What would you do without me?"

"This is a special announcement," the radio blared. "President Genus has declared January 20th a national holiday. During this day of remembrance, mourning, and celebration, citizens are required to remain in their resident dwellings. Inter-dwelling gatherings are prohibited. Businesses will shutter at midnight on January 19th and remain closed until noon on January 21st. The televised event will culminate with President Genus' address to the nation. Viewing is mandatory and will be monitored. Your government thanks you for your understanding during these troublesome times. For the betterment of us all, control your soul's desire for freedom until the threat to your safety has passed."

Jack turned to UW. The man's smile held malice.

"They never disappoint. In case you missed it, Jack, that was the beginning."

CHAPTER 43

PREDAWN, JANUARY 19TH, STINGER MACHINERY

Crestwater's Prius jumped the curb and screeched to a stop on Stinger Machinery's walkway. He burst from the interior and rushed towards Jack who awaited him flanked by three BHR agents.

"Follow me," Jack yelled as he turned to enter the building.

"If this is an attempt at humor, Mister Stinger, I'll have you arrested immediately." Crestwater hurried to catch up with Jack, focused solely on the entrance. "Keep a diligent eye out for suspicious persons," he yelled as he passed the agents and entered the building.

Jack stood with his back to the door, staring at the damage. The walls had been ripped out and electric wiring dangled between heavy wooden framing.

"My word! What happened?" Crestwater gasped.

"It gets worse. Look at the floor."

Agent Crestwater squinted in the dim light, searching the debris. "What am I looking for?"

"That powdery stuff isn't dirt. It runs all the way to the parking lot."

Struck by realization, Crestwater recoiled, then followed the powdery trail through the lobby into the office.

"We've been robbed, haven't we?"

"Yes," Jack said, nodding. "A large amount of powder, machines, and components were taken. It appears they tried their hand at manufacturing, then decided it'd be easier to just pilfer everything."

Horror dominated Crestwater's features. A breach such as this would surely end his career. He pushed past Jack and rushed into the shop area. His head bowed, and he sobbed softly as the emptiness overwhelmed him.

"I have some good news," Jack said.

Crestwater's head shot up, hope filling his eyes.

"It looks like one of them was injured when they broke the lock on the powder container. We should be able to get a DNA sample. It won't take long to identify the thieves. I had the BHR agents call a forensics team. They're en route."

Crestwater searched for traces of blood but found nothing. "Jack, what are you talking about? I observe no blood, lock, or other clues to aid our apprehension of the thieves."

"It's inside. Mind your step around the powder. I'm sure the forensics team will want to examine it, too."

Crestwater realized the powder trail led through the entire building and ended somewhere inside the trailer. He joined Jack a moment later but found no trace of the evidence Jack had promised existed.

"Agent, in roughly fifteen minutes, you're going to wish you'd had the fire suppression system installed. Oh, you'll also regret using these stupid fucking shipping containers instead of building an actual storage room, you know. One that has door handles on both sides."

Agent Crestwater's brow furrowed as he worked his way through Jack's meaning. As understanding struck, shock consumed him. He moved to escape only to be slammed to the container's metal floor. The impact forced the air from his lungs and dimmed his vision.

Jack zip-cuffed Crestwater's feet and hands together, hogtying the nearly unconscious agent. "Yep, you really should have installed that fire suppression system. But, if you think about it, it wouldn't help. The explosion will kill you, not the fire. It's how it worked for the BHR agents at my house. You know, the house your government took from me and gave to you. You got lucky when those idiots showed up. In retrospect, your survival made my life easier."

***

Crestwater's frantic pleas went unanswered. He tried to wriggle free of his restraints to no avail. He rested his face on the floor and sobbed. The overhead light suddenly blazed to life. Hope swelled within him. Someone had arrived to liberate him! Jack certainly wouldn't have turned the lights on; the man was a sadist. Leaving Crestwater in empty blackness was more his style.

"Please, help! Hurry, they plan to blow me up!"

A second ticked by before he realized he'd heard no sound from his rescuers. He strained to turn his head towards the door. They hadn't heard his desperate cries. It startled him to see two men seated against the wall, unnoticed in the dark, their presence undeniable in the stark light.

"Thank the higher power. Untie me. We must flee this place at once."

Neither man moved, their unblinking eyes fixed on some unseen object.

"I said, untie me. We're in grave danger!"

Nothing. Neither man moved.

Crestwater studied them. They were both dressed in clothing similar to what Jack and Willis donned most days and wearing limited essential passes.

"Are you the thieves? I promise I'll not seek prosecution of your deeds if you release me."

He tried blinking away the sweat blurring his vision, squinted, then focused on their faces. Maybe Jack had clubbed them into a daze. He gasped when he noticed a trickle of blood escaping a ragged hole in the larger man's forehead.

***

"Everything's loaded. Whenever you're ready," UW said as he removed the BHR helmet and tossed it into the trailer hitched to the BHR sedan.

Jack stared at the contents until his uncle placed a hand on his shoulder.

"I told you, your father was a wise man. We'll be able to use those guns at the lodge. They're a bit heavy to lug around the streets."

"They're beautiful," Jack responded, still staring at the half dozen M1 rifles resting in long-term storage bags. "When did he hide them? Why inside the walls of Stinger Machinery?"

"A long time ago. He figured the government would never think to search for guns at a machine shop."

"We should probably wrap this up. Sunrise is in twenty minutes, and you have a long ride ahead of you," Mathews interrupted as Randy stepped next to Jack and nodded.

As the others prepared to leave, Jack stared at Stinger Machinery. The building that held his most cherished memories would soon cease to exist. He pulled his government cell phone from his tactical vest and powered it on. When it screeched to life, he punched in the number for the Citizen Soldiers Cleveland Division.

"This is Jack Stinger," he shouted. "Stinger Machinery is being robbed! Send help! Me, Willis Stinger, and Agent Crestwater are going inside the building to stop the thieves. Please hurry!" He ended the call, tossed the phone at the building, set a matchbook ablaze, and tossed it onto the gunpowder trail.

The hazy morning sky flashed a brilliant orange in the rearview mirror. The concussion reached them an instant later. Stinger Machinery was gone, ending in a brilliant fireball. Jack knew his father would approve.

His reverie broke when UW's sat-phone buzzed. His uncle read the message aloud: "Red sky in morning." He smiled at Jack's questioning gaze. "Emmitt just disrupted food distribution to most of Northeast Ohio. No turning back now."

Chapter 44

January 19th,
Andrews Air Force Base

Governor Dunbar awoke with a start, jostled to consciousness by Governor Sloan.

"How much did you drink?" she asked, observing her friend's disorientation.

"Not much, but enough. Are we still in the air? I specifically told you not to wake me until we landed," he blurted, panic creeping into his voice.

"Holy shit," Sloan laughed. "You truly hate flying, don't you? We've landed and are taxiing to the hangar. Go to the bathroom and freshen up. Maybe reapply your deodorant. Your *not much to drink* is bleeding through your pores."

Groggy from sleep and several double Crown Royals, Dunbar surveyed his surroundings. The plush couch along the wall of Air Force One's conference room had proved a comfortable makeshift bed during the short flight from Newark. There, the surviving governors met to board Air Force One and fly to Andrews Air Force Base. He wasn't in a hurry to surrender the couch or stand up.

"I'll shower at the hotel," he said, watching the grounds of Andrews flash by the windows. "Where are we deplaning?"

"The hanger. We deplane, board busses to the EEOB, and meet Woods and Cummings. We won't arrive at the hotel until late tonight. Please, freshen up now. You'll stink to high heaven by that time."

Air Force One turned left sharply. Harsh fluorescent brightness suddenly replaced the natural light filtering into the cabin.

"Ladies and gentlemen, this is your captain speaking. You will deplane through the front and rear hatches."

The announcement, void of pleasantries, ended as abruptly as it began as the plane jerked to a stop.

***

Resignation set in as he descended the stairs. No busses awaited them, only large military cargo trucks surrounded by dozens of armed BHR agents. He watched, horrified, as the BHR corralled the governors who'd disembarked before him towards the trucks and forced them into their cargo holds, their demands and objections simply ignored.

As he boarded and struggled to find an unoccupied space to stand, a bullhorn screeched to life.

"You are being transferred to a Bureau of Harm Reduction holding facility. Upon arrival, we will begin our investigation. Understand that your government frowns on treason and will punish those found guilty of such heinous crimes severely."

Dunbar's lips trembled. His attempt to smile failed as he stared into his friend's eyes. "You were right. I should have stayed in Ohio."

Chapter 45

Eight Hours Prior To National Address, January 20th, IX Center

"How many bodies? Did you identify them?" Wolfe yelled at his computer's monitor.

"Sir, the computer can't hear you. Hence, Representative Woods' admin, who authored the email, likewise cannot hear or respond," Veronica said, after recovering from Wolfe's flinch-inducing reaction to the news about Stinger Machinery.

Wolfe glared at her. "Tread lightly, Veronica."

"Sorry, sir, I thought maybe you assumed your voice recognition editing program was active," she lied. "I'll point out that regardless of Willis and Jack Stinger's deaths, Woods approved your Form 85FAR. Although Lisa Stinger wasn't your primary target, she may still be hiding in the Stinger dwelling, defenseless."

Wolfe's expression told her he hadn't considered this twist. "I wanted them all behind bars. Death's too easy," he snipped, cheeks flushing with embarrassment.

"Of course, sir. Shall I, on your behalf, advise Squads Four and Six to prepare to execute the Form 85FAR?"

"Not yet. We're on hold until after Genus' speech, but have both squad leaders report to me A-SAP."

"I'll get with them directly, sir. Oh, and don't forget to put your armband on. Today's the day—you'll be fined if you're caught without it."

"That doesn't go into effect until after Genus' speech later this afternoon."

"You're correct, sir, but you'll be deployed when she finishes her national address, as will your troops. The Squad Leaders have already directed their teams to wear them. You should follow their example." When she finished, Veronica held up her arm to show Wolfe she was wearing hers.

Wolfe, again struck by the imagery the armbands resembled, said, "Did you notice anything odd about the bands?"

"Other than being flimsy garbage?"

"No—well, they *are* garbage. But I'm talking about what they resemble. The Nazis wore similar armbands."

Veronica started at the mention of Nazi armbands. She'd missed the resemblance.

"Now that you mention it, they do. It must be an oversight. Our leadership would never knowingly align with such brutality."

***

Wolfe stood facing the whiteboard, sketching a diagram of West 11th with the target dwelling circled in red.

"We hit the instant Genus concludes her speech. Be sure every member of your team watches it from inside the LAVs. They're monitoring viewership and no one is exempt."

He drew a sloppy representation of Lincoln Park, adding a large red arrow pointing directly at the target dwelling.

"Squad Four," he announced, locking eyes with SL Jones. "Your team makes first contact. Enter the park from 14th and double-time to the dwelling. The ground will be muddy. If you get bogged down, deploy immediately from your position of last progress. Set up a four-man perimeter and send the other four into the dwelling. Engage hostiles on contact."

Not waiting for a response, he added another arrow, this one pointing north from Starkweather Avenue.

"Squad Six," he said, glancing over his shoulder at SL Fletch. "When Jones confirms entry, you move into position a dwelling south of our target. Send four agents to the rear of the dwelling and four to support Jones' breaching team. I'll hold position on 14th. After your teams secure the dwelling, I'll join you. Questions?"

"Sir," Fletch said. "Define hostile."

Wolfe grinned. "Aside from Lisa Stinger, anyone inside that dwelling."

CHAPTER 46

SEVEN HOURS PRIOR TO NATIONAL ADDRESS, JANUARY 20TH,
TREMONT

Mathews looped the fishing line around the perimeter security device's safety pin and released it slowly. The 12-gauge shell would spray the area with steel shot when it detonated, something he wanted to avoid while he was kneeling next to it. He'd positioned the tripwire-activated device facing the entrance from the garage. It would shred anyone entering the house and alert Mathews to the intrusion.

He stood, admiring his work. The tiny hallway connecting the garage and kitchen was now an inescapable kill box. He and Randy—communicating by writing on notepads—determined the old school booby-trap would prevent the BHR from flanking them.

"Mathews for Lisa."

"Go for Lisa."

"The last perimeter device is in place. Let Max's team know we have shot-shells in the following locations: front porch, two feet from the entrance; north and south sides of the house, three feet from the east-facing exterior wall corners; interior garage, facing the overhead door; backyard, eight feet from the south-facing corner; and interior garage door when entering the house. How copy?"

"Good copy," Lisa responded. After a brief pause, she said, "UW and Jack have confirmed they're in place and standing by." She bit her lip, worried about Mathews' answer to her next question. "How's Randy? Any problems with communication?"

"Dicey at first, but we figured it out. When this is over, you'll need to teach me sign language. The guy's a freaking tank. He's moving the furniture while I set the tripwires and hasn't asked for any help. He created a maze at the entrance with the kitchen table flipped on its side five yards in. Whoever gets past the tripwire immediately enters the maze and becomes an easy target. The scrap metal sheets Willis supplied should provide him with decent protection when this kicks off. For my position, he bolted the leftover metal to Willis' coffee table in the living room. I'll have a clear view of the front yard and porch."

"I figured he'd be in his element," Lisa said, relief washing over her. "I understand you don't know him well, but he's solid. How are you holding up? My offer to trade places still stands."

"Nah. I'm Army, I'll be fine. Plus, I have a handful of aspirin to nurse me along. You just make sure Max's crew is prepared to move if this goes sideways."

"We've got two shooters in the tower. Me, Max, and Watt are setting up on top of the pool house. I'll be able to hit you with a rock or, more likely, rescue the big tough Army man in a flash."

Her barb elicited shared, yet subdued, laughter. An uneasy silence replaced the moment of levity.

"Tonight, we start taking our country back. I *will* see you for EVAC at nineteen-hundred."

"Copy that. Stinger, out."

Chapter 47

**Thirty Minutes Prior To National Address,
January 20th,
EEOB**

Major General Stein's four-man security detail closed ranks around him as they exited the LAV that had transported him from the Pentagon to the front steps of the Eisenhower Executive Office Building.

His meeting with Genus, scheduled to begin directly after her address, afforded him the rare opportunity to witness a presidential address in person, something he wished had happened under different circumstances. The strap of his messenger-style briefcase cutting into his shoulder was a stark reminder of his meeting's topic.

As the elevator door parted, a contingent of Secret Service agents buttressed by two squads of BHR agents in full battle-rattle greeted them.

"General Stein, I'll need to see your invitation and pass," one of the SS said as Stein stepped into the hall leading to the auditorium. "Huh. Does everyone in DC have a personal security detail these days?" he asked as he glanced over Steins' shoulder.

"Papers and pass," Stein said, waving a stack of documents. "You'll find the same for these idiots," he growled, bobbing his head towards his entourage. "To answer your question, I didn't want or need security. However, I had no choice. I'm sure you understand."

The agent smirked as an inside joke passed between them. "Got it. They'll need to take their aviators off for positive ID."

"Gentlemen, you heard the agent. Take those ridiculous glasses off and smile pretty."

The SS agent compared each Bureau of Harm Reduction identification badge to the corresponding essential person pass, then held them next to the appropriate agent's face, ensuring the picture matched.

"I thought you military types didn't appreciate facial hair on your staff?" he asked, referring to the bushy mustaches covering the upper lip of two of the BHR agents.

"They're not my staff. One Marine could replace these wannabes but Marines are in short supply. So, I'm stuck with Disco Stu and his misfits."

"Down the hall," the agent said through restrained laughter. "You're assigned seats in the back of the auditorium. President Genus will send for you after her national address."

***

Stein glanced around the expansive auditorium and realized the only faces he recognized belonged to his long-time military colleagues. He marveled at the speed with which Eden's administration had eliminated an entire generation of politicians and did so with nary a soul fighting back. Focusing on the members of the military, he realized they were the only attendees accompanied by security details.

"Arrogant, undisciplined pricks," he whispered as he watched dozens of gray-suited bureaucrats scurry about, offering congratulations to one another and free of the oppressive guards they had saddled his friends with. The cause of the nearly jubilant behavior had escaped Stein, but he speculated Genus' speech would answer that question.

A loud bang pulled his attention to the stage and sent dozens of gray-suited bureaucrats into a mild panic. His brow furrowed at the sight of a maintenance team struggling with a protective barrier. One of the three heavy clear acrylic slabs had gotten away from them and crashed to the stage.

"Well," he whispered. "I didn't expect that."

Chapter 48

January 20th, Tremont

Randy studied the video feed from his drone. He'd identified three LAVs idling in the school to the west, putting them at the rear of their location. Only a row of homes butting up to UW's property separated them. As he watched, a fourth LAV arrived, escorted by two of the smaller armored vehicles the Citizen Soldiers had employed until recently.

He raised his hand above the kitchen table's edge, signaling to Mathews the number had grown. Mathews pounded on the floor, the vibration confirming to Randy he'd received the update. The BHR and CS force was growing. He quickly updated Lisa and she informed him an additional LAV had arrived west of Lincoln Park, joining three already in position for thirty minutes. He was starting to worry.

Glancing at his watch, he realized Genus' address would start any minute and powered on the television.

***

"Go," Max yelled, sending Lisa and Watt charging across West 14th. He took the position at their six and was on their heels within seconds. After crossing the street, they held at a location behind a hedgerow and waited to see if they'd been spotted. From that point, they'd be able to use the brush as cover until they made it to the swimming pool twenty-five yards away.

With the overcast sun low in the western sky, visibility was dropping rapidly. It provided them the additional cover they needed to break towards the pool. Max held them for seven minutes, then ordered them to move.

Watt arrived first. He knelt and laced his fingers for Lisa to use as a boost to reach the low-slung roof of the pool house. Max soon followed, turning to help Watt scale the distance. They waited, crouched and motionless, straining to hear, searching for any indication the LAVs had seen them.

Max twirled a hand above his head, sending them to their assigned positions where they readied for their first target to present itself.

***

"Lisa for Mathews."

"Go for Mathews."

"We're in position. Clear sightlines to your position. Area is quiet."

"Roger that. Randy reports another squad has arrived east of our position. We're monitoring the BHR radios. Minimal chatter."

"This is Max. Have him scan the area to our south. Report findings A-SAP. Keep that radio on. Notify us of any movement towards our position."

"Roger," Mathews answered after a brief pause. "Glassing our southern flank."

"Mathews for Lisa."

"Go for Lisa."

"I have a question. How big is Willis' cabin? I really don't want to bunk with you again."

"Mathews, I might shoot you myself. The property holds six small cabins and the main cabin. Although your ugly ass will be sleeping in the woods if I have anything to say about it."

"Genus' address is starting. I'll update you on Randy's findings. Also, Lisa, the woods would be a welcome change. I'm sure nothing in nature snores like you. Mathews, out."

Lisa heard soft laughter from Max and Watt.

"You know," Watt said. "He isn't wrong. You can definitely saw a log."

Lisa's head sank to the moss-covered roof. "Don't, Watt. Just don't."

Chapter 49

January 20th, EEOB

Stein smirked as Representatives Woods and Cummings took the stage. Their appearance hadn't caused his insolent smile. The exaggerated, cultish response of the elites had been its catalyst. He feared the auditorium would implode as President Genus joined them. The thunderous applause rattled his seat as she stepped up to the podium, smiling at her adoring subordinates.

Glancing down, she appeared confused. Her head shot up and she searched the crowd. Her quarry unknown but her panic spoke to its importance.

"She's already lost," Woods whispered. "We should have stayed with our original plan and kept her isolated. Putting her in front of a live audience is suicide."

Cummings nodded her agreement. "We do as we're told. She'll be dealt with soon enough. Until then, smile a politician's smile. Mister Rosos is watching."

"There you are," Genus said, her cackling laughter blaring from the speakers.

Stein followed her gaze. She'd located her lifeline, a teleprompter positioned directly in front of the stage. How she'd

OA: Consent of the Governed

missed it became clear as her image suddenly appeared on an enormous wall-mounted monitor at the rear of the stage. Dilated pupils and slack features spoke of a woman heavily sedated.

"Before we start and broadcast this historic speech to every citizen across the country, I want to thank you for attending. In these troublesome times, your presence demonstrates courage and shows your deep yearning to right the wrongs of our country's checkered history. You've leaned into the challenges, open-faced and resilient, while battling to transform our administration's visions to life."

The room exploded. Gray suits from every branch of government sprang to their feet, screaming their approval of Genus' praise. Her features morphed into a scrunched smile as she motioned for her minions to let her continue.

"I'd be remiss if I didn't recognize two exceptional women. Without their steadfast commitment, loyalty, and understanding, I would not be standing here today." Genus' tone had taken on a childlike tenor as if sharing a fairytale. "I ask you to recognize Representatives Woods and Cummings, the ladies holding our country together!" Genus was screeching as she finished, trying to be heard above the exuberant gray suits.

Genus gestured for the audience to be seated, then placed a hand to her ear, struggling to hear a message from some unseen source. A mad, distorted smile took over her features.

"Your attention, please. Our broadcast is beginning. Prepare to step into the future!"

Chapter 50

January 20th, Tremont

Genus' glassy-eyed visage had just filled the television when Randy raised his hand, signaling the addition of two LAVs to the government forces amassing throughout their neighborhood.

The force to their south appeared light by comparison, pointing to a wave-type assault on the city's nonessential population. Max and Mathews understood the tactical miscalculation. It was pure arrogance—a feeling of invincibility—and would cost the government dearly.

"Max, Randy indicates two additional squads. Keep your head on a swivel. It's getting thick," Mathews said in a low voice.

"Roger that. Keep monitoring their radios and advise. Has Genus' address started?"

"Affirmative. Will advise you of its conclusion."

Mathews raised his helmet's boom microphone and increased the volume of the BHR radio. It was deathly quiet.

"My fellow Americans," Genus' voice refocused his attention on the television. "I'm sure, after a full day of tributes to President Eden, your souls are jubilant. Our sincerest thanks go to our broadcast partners for a job well done. What a great man he was!"

Genus' effectual pause outlived her handler's patience as she jerked her hand to her ear again, then refocused on the camera.

"However, we must share news which you may find difficult to hear. Yesterday, acting on Bureau of Civic Responsibility intelligence, the Bureau of Harm Reduction arrested our country's surviving state governors. Please do not allow this to dampen your spirits. This action was part of our constantly evolving strategy to ensure your safety. Our intelligence community discovered a coup plot hatched by none other than Chief of Staff Roberts who, as you'll recall, played a key role in the assassination of our beloved President Eden. At the time of Eden's murder, we were unaware of the conspiracy's depth. Its web was tangled in every corner of our beautiful nation. If not for the valiant efforts of our BCR, we may never have uncovered the coconspirators, allowing them to roam free to plan their next attack upon your government. Rest assured, they will be dealt with!"

***

A deep thumping drew Stein's attention from the stage. He searched for the source as its intensity grew. It shocked him to find the gray suits stamping their feet in perfect rhythm. He recognized its purpose—a modern version of a battle drum.

"I share your enthusiasm and wrap my arms around your support," Genus said, refocusing them on her. "On to a lighter, more joyful topic," she slurred as her eyelids seemed unwilling to remain open. "For these last two years, your government—in tandem with our business partners—stumbled upon a startling revelation. While observing you in your natural habitat, it has become obvious you've been living incorrectly. You've incorrectly pursued financial security, failed to control your soul's desire for autonomy, and incorrectly placed your needs over those of your government. Your mistake was not recognizing your government can provide these things for you … because we care."

***

Mathew's backbone stiffened. Genus had lost her mind. "Are you hearing this shit?" he whispered into his radio.

"Negative," Lisa answered. "Has she wrapped up?" She tightened her grip on the M4 resting on its bipod in front of her.

"Negative, but she is bat-shit crazy. I'm having Randy pull the drone back. Stay frosty."

Mathews slammed on the floor to get Randy's attention. He held up his hand and slowly clenched it into a fist. Randy nodded and quickly disappeared behind the upended table.

"However, to achieve our goal," Genus mumbled, losing her battle with the opiates racing through her system, "we must labor as one to build a government which can support you, provide for you, and care for you. I'm sure you've asked yourself how much harder must you toil supporting those who refuse to pledge their loyalty to our government? The answer is no harder than you labor today because your government is here to help. At the conclusion of today's festivities, your government will begin relocating all nonessentials to enlightenment camps. Upon arrival, their labor therapy begins. We will cure them of their Free Man Syndrome, train them in the arts of sanitation management, environmental cleanliness, workplace curator, and much more. Upon completion of the program, they will be assigned to a place of labor to perform their newly acquired skills, lessening the burden on those of you who've demonstrated loyalty through your thoughts and actions."

Chapter 51

January 20th,
Enlightenment Camp Alpha, Mojave Desert

Dale turned to face Margaux, her sharp gasp causing him concern about her emotional wellbeing.

"What's wrong?" he whispered, hoping to avoid the scrutiny of the guards stationed next to the monitor. "Have Genus' words triggered a repressed emotion?"

Margaux grasped Dale's hand, squeezing it tight. "No, it provoked comprehension," she whispered. "The soon arriving guests will consist solely of nonessentials. Their station in life deemed a crime. Instead of encouraging them into our ideology, Genus plans to thrust it upon them. This is an action that will unquestionably breed contempt and resentment, pushing them further from Eden's righteous vision. Our long-term goal will fail."

"I appreciate your concern. However, they've sown their fields through free will. In my judgment, they'll provide excellent cannon fodder as we set our strategy in motion."

Margaux drifted as Genus droned on. The President's mannerisms had always caused her to detach from the moment. The woman could be insufferable.

Dale was correct. Nonessentials had invited this outcome; she would put it to good use. Running through the timeline and adjusting for time zones, Margaux determined the inaugural arrivals would undoubtedly hail from western states. The flow of new detainees would stretch on for days, possibly weeks, as hundreds of thousands of nonessentials arrived.

"Dale, it becomes a matter of resources. This action will overextend our government. They will focus on our camp and others like it. However, the transport vehicles will be staffed with a minimal security force. Assuming Spangler has been truthful and the south gate is rendered unguarded, driving a transport through the fencing seems a less dangerous undertaking than rushing it en masse. The uprising we initiate will distract camp security, rendering the transports easily commandeered."

"Forever the thinker, my friend. We must spread the word of our tactical modification at the conclusion of today's events."

"No talking!" a guard screamed as he glared at them. "Do not disrespect our dear leader."

Margaux's grip on Dale's hand tightened, her fear of being sent to solitary confinement nearly uncontrollable. She faced her friend, their eyes locked, a silent message passing. Their plan would work. It simply had to.

CHAPTER 52

JANUARY 20TH, CAMP LEJEUNE

Sergeant Bixby watched, dumbfounded, as the gray suits' wild applause drowned out President Genus. Their enthusiasm at hearing the President's nonessential solution sent ice through his veins as his resolve strengthened.

His attention was drawn to the Marines crowded into the Marston Pavilion's Tinian Hall. Camp Lejeune's remaining contingent of four hundred warfighters were able to assemble with no threat of overcrowding.

"Our solution will sever the terrorists' lifeline!" Genus screamed to be heard and refocused Bixby's attention on the monitor. "It will eliminate their ability to recruit amongst this pool of mental defects professing their misguided patriotism."

The gray suits' raucous cheering again forced Genus to pause. The President's knees appeared to buckle, her faltering barely noticeable as she struggled to remove something from the breast pocket of her gray suit coat.

"Furthermore, a solution has been developed for two separate yet equally important challenges."

She fell silent, continuing to search her pocket for something which appeared pivotal to her next statement.

"Where are you?" she mumbled. "Ah, found you," she screeched triumphantly as she raised her hand above her head. "This device conquers a challenge you're probably brutally aware of: our monetary system!"

The broadcast jumped and shook as the camera struggled to track the President's gesticulating hand. She placed her free hand to her ear, nodded, and suddenly stopped moving, allowing the camera to focus on a clear, matchbook-sized box. Its contents, barely larger than a grain of rice, rested in black foam.

"Effective immediately, hard currency is illegal. Not only does it pose a burden to places of business, it enables those intending to inflict harm upon you to purchase the supplies necessary to sustain their terror campaign undetected. This chip contains your pertinent data. Once implanted beneath the skin in the webbing of your thumb, a plethora of opportunities will unfold. Your labor earnings will be recorded on the chip. Payments for goods and services become as easy as waving your hand. Your health will be monitored, allowing medical professionals to schedule appointments for you before you're even aware an illness is coursing through your body. The benefits are endless!"

Bixby's eyes widened. The dystopian future Genus had strived to achieve was coming to fruition. With a tiny slice of your skin, government would control every aspect of your life.

A hush fell over Tinian Hall. The shock caused by Genus' words visible on the face of every Marine watching her address.

Bixby reached to his ankle and unfastened the strap securing the pistol hidden beneath his BDU's pant leg. The sound of diesel engines caught his interest. As he strained to hear, the reality materialized. The machines gathering outside were Light Armored Vehicles and they were surrounding Tinian Hall. This was a development he and his team had not prepared for but would adapt to.

Chapter 53

January 20th, EEOB

"Relax," Stein growled as his security detail shifted anxiously. "Remain focused on the President's address. Remember, it's an honor to be here."

"Your enthusiasm encourages me," Genus said, responding to her minions' feral applause. "It shows you understand and embrace our goals."

Her head bobbed, then rose sharply. Despite her consciousness faltering, she plowed forward. "Life Chipping, as we have named it, begins on February 1st. No doubt you've recognized that Life Chipping the entire populace will be a monumental undertaking, particularly in the midst of the war for our country's very soul. Your concern brings me to my next exceedingly important topic. Although your government remains strong, these troublesome times have exacted a heavy toll. We've scrutinized our options and found the answer to be obvious—literally in front of us. To demonstrate, I ask you to turn to face those around you." Genus paused, waiting as the crowd obliged her request. "You see, we are a multicultural society; a tapestry of experiences, races, and nationalities. We realized a simple truth. Our borders stretch far beyond the geographical boundaries we've labored—actually, *hidden behind* for hundreds of years. This moment of illumination electrified our thinking and brought the power of social unity to bear. At that instant, our country's structure began to mold, shift, and realign. We understood a simple truth: requesting assistance from other countries was equivalent to asking for the help of the American people themselves."

Anticipating yet another clamorous response, Genus hushed. She recoiled at the awkward silence, her features morphing through dozens of expressions before landing on confusion.

"Maybe I should clarify," she blurted, concentrating mightily on the voice in her earpiece. "We have erased our borders and requested assistance from a multinational alliance. Your government asks you not to be startled by the presence of soldiers from what we once considered foreign countries on our soil. Remind yourself that they had already been here, their culture represented by your friends and neighbors. This simple fact gives them claim to our country, one we will now employ, lean on, to end these troublesome times."

Stein's focus shifted to Woods and Cummings seated slightly behind Genus and flanking her on either side. The women had remained stoic until the gray suits faltered in their support of Genus. Each glared into the crowd; a message of consequence delivered and responded to with subdued applause.

"That's what I thought," Stein whispered. "None of you saw this coming. You're expendable."

Chapter 54

January 20th,
Billy's LAV, South Tremont Patrol

Sensing Genus was wrapping up, Billy exited his Light Armored Vehicle through the overhead turret.

"I'm going to recon the area. I have a feeling we'll be kicking off soon," he said, answering Rodriguez's questioning stare.

He felt the eyes of a frightened neighborhood on him as he walked to the rear of the LAV, removed his government cell, and dialed his father. His call went to voicemail. It didn't matter if the government overheard his message, he'd soon be a hunted man regardless.

"Hey, Dad. Sorry I missed you. You're probably still watching Genus' train wreck. Um ... it's important you know I did the right thing. No matter what they say, you can be proud of me, Dad. I've gotta go," he said, clearing his throat. "I love you."

Billy turned off his phone and tossed it into the early evening haze. As he reached the hatch, he slid his sidearm from its holster, performed a press check, then reentered the LAV.

"Looks like she's wrapping up," Rodriguez said as Billy took the driver's seat.

Billy nodded. "She is, and we're about to unleash a shitstorm. Were you able to talk to your family before we rolled out?"

"Yeah. My wife's a mess, but the baby's keeping her busy. Thank God for that. How about you?"

"Nope," Billy said, the word bitter on his tongue. "Yang was in a mood. He kept leadership at HQ locked down tight. Tried my dad a couple times today, but we never connected."

"Excuse me, gentlemen. We're trying to watch the President! Please refrain from speaking or I'll report you for dereliction of duty and interfering with a mandatory government broadcast," Thatcher whined from the troop hold where the squad sat huddled around their phones.

"Thatch. First, fuck you. Second, lock your beady little eyes on your phone. I'll be quizzing you when it ends," Billy shot back.

"Here it comes, Thatcher. Hurry or you'll miss it," one of his squadmates squealed.

Chapter 55

OA, Day One, EEOB

As Genus reached her crescendo, Stein unbuttoned his dress blues jacket. The pistol secured in his shoulder holster didn't need to be checked. He knew a round was chambered.

The President raised her arms in victory as she shouted against the deafening roar. "We are one! We will remain one! We have erased our country's borders, our state borders. We are no longer encumbered by interstate rivalries. No longer will one state succeed at the cost of another. No longer will you be forced to deal with confusing and contradictory laws from one jurisdiction to the next! Our national police force—a merger of our BHR and BCR—will dispense even-handed, equal justice. We have achieved the comfort of social unification!"

Genus stumbled backward, her raised arms proving too much for her opiate-compromised equilibrium. Woods shot from her chair, steadying Genus and guiding her back to the podium.

"You've done well, now wrap it up," she whispered into the President's ear.

Gripping the sides of the podium, Genus moved to end her address and unleash the first night of One America.

"Your new Regional Assistant Leaders will introduce themselves during local town hall events." She turned to ensure the RAL's portraits were displayed on the monitor. "These fine men are Regional Assistant Leaders Ong, Pan, Shen, and Tsang. Please welcome them with open arms. Now, I leave you with this." Again, she raised her arms in victory. "Welcome to our new America. Welcome to One America!"

As she spoke, a giant flag unfurled behind her displaying an eagle holding a single star.

Stein drew a sharp breath as the soldier to his right sent a one-word text message. "NOW!"

Chapter 56

OA, Day One,
Multiple Locations

Mathews watched as the feed from Genus cut to static. Several black lines rolled up the screen, then Jack appeared with Willis and Stein in dress blues standing behind him.

"Shit's on," Mathews reported calmly into his radio as the prerecorded video dominated the airwaves. He slammed on the floor twice, focusing Randy on the front door. His battle rifle peeking above the upended table, leveled and ready.

"Ladies and gentlemen, my name is Jack Stinger. Like you, I've lost everything I once held dear. I watched as our beautiful country transformed into a dystopian reality. Eden's administration guaranteed us equality. Yet, they divided us by our worth to their machine, labeling and separating us by our essential status. They assured you prosperity, yet nationalized American businesses, rendering you a serf to government's apparatus. They promised us a fair and just society but have imprisoned your friends and family for having the audacity to think freely, disagree, and choose self-reliance. They lied! Look out your window. Those vehicles of war you see, they're coming for you. Eventually, they'll come for us all. Government has forgotten it exists with our consent. We the people are the masters of our destinies. I implore you to join us as we take our country back. We have declared war. We have defined a temporary leadership structure and we will end their tyranny. You no longer have the option to be a bystander; this war will touch everyone. To my nonessential friends, it's time!"

***

"Cut the feed, cut the feed, cut the goddamned feed!" Woods screamed into her radio as Cummings rushed Genus from the stage.

"Let's roll," Stein barked as he stood.

Jack and UW were moving the instant Stein spoke, heading to intercept Genus. They pushed through the building chaos of the EEOB. Steps from the stage, a voice rose above the din.

"Ladies and gentlemen, shut up and sit down. You are under arrest for treason."

Jack risked a glance over his shoulder. Stein now stood at the podium, flanked by the two remaining members of his security detail. His order sent the gray suits scrambling for the exits.

"This way," UW yelled as he jumped over seatbacks, heading for a gap in the crowd, his fake mustache falling free.

Jack followed his uncle's lead. "I've lost the target. Do you have eyes on her?"

He spun when UW failed to answer and spotted Willis as he crushed the bridge of a gray suit's nose with his rifle.

"Move, Jack! They can't get behind that door. If they do, it's over."

Jack followed UW's gaze. Twenty feet away, he found Woods, Cummings, and Genus bottlenecked at the emergency exit; hundreds of gray suits forced their way past them as they tried to escape the growing pandemonium. Jack's rage-filled eyes locked on Woods.

"I'm coming for you!" he screamed.

Chapter 57

OA, Day One,
Tremont South Patrol

Seated in the cab, Billy lowered the rear troop door.

"Move your asses," he yelled at his squad, who'd frozen in place watching the events unfolding in the EEOB. He was sending them to their death and wanted to get it over with.

Thatcher stood, his jaw squared, muscles flexing with anger.

"We end these dregs tonight! Follow me into battle," he yelled as he raced toward the rear hatch, his squadmates on his heels.

Billy buried his head in his arms as gunfire erupted in the troop hold.

"Do you trust me now?" Rodriguez asked as he dropped the empty magazine from his smoking M4.

Billy grinned. "You did me a favor. Take a seat. We've got someplace to be."

The top of Rodriguez's head exploded as he stepped toward the cab. Billy took cover as the gun's report echoed through the troop hold.

"I knew you were a traitor," Thatcher seethed, his right arm hanging limp at his side, blood dripping from his fingertips. "Tonight, I exact my revenge."

He scrambled up the troop ramp, rushing toward Billy, gun leading his crazed eyes. One shot, another, then a third rang out. The bullets ricocheted off the thick steel plate separating the driver from the troop hold.

"You can't hide forever, you vile creature," he fumed as he stalked toward the cab. Mere feet from his target, he slipped in Rodriguez's pooling blood. His arm flailed as he tried to regain balance, but he quickly slammed to his back. The impact sent his gun skittering away.

"Thatcher, stop talking like a douche," Billy chided, suddenly filling the gap between the front seats. His Glock leveled at Thatcher's head. "It's why people never liked you."

The .40 caliber round smashed through the bridge of Thatcher's nose, ending his life on the troop hold's cold steel floor.

Porch lights joined interior lights, flashing a message of unity throughout the neighborhood as Billy shifted the LAV into gear. He left the bodies where they lay. He was running out of time.

CHAPTER 58

OA, DAY ONE, WILLIS STINGER'S HOME

Mathews heard the engines roar a moment before the church tower snipers called out, "Hostiles advancing!"

He rose above the makeshift bunker, glanced at Randy, and nodded.

"Dear Lord, guide my hand," Mathews whispered. "Keep my aim true and forgive me my sins. Also, I'm not ready yet, so I would appreciate anything you can do to delay our meeting."

As if adding an exclamation point to his prayer, the north tripwire detonated. Agonized screams quickly followed the blast as buckshot found flesh.

"Tripwire! Watch for booby traps—"

The warning, blaring from the BHR radio Mathews was monitoring, was cut off when the porch tripwire detonated, quickly followed by gunfire.

"Squad Six, move to support. Now! Squad Four, advance on that dwelling!"

Boots slapping on wood told Mathews that a breaching team was on the porch. Gritting his teeth against the looming pain, he pulled the trigger, spraying bullets through the porch-facing window, cutting down the lead soldier.

"Covering fire! We need covering fire!" a panic-filled voice screamed over the radio.

Mathews slid to the floor, his chest screaming for vengeance. "Lisa, heads up. They're calling for covering fire. You've been spotted."

"Negative," Lisa replied. "We haven't fired. They're in a panic, shooting at shadows. Stay low. They're going to spray the house."

The south tripwire detonated, cutting Lisa off.

"Number of remaining hostiles?" Mathews asked.

"Two. Front of house, using a vehicle as cover. Second LAV en route," Lisa answered, her tone ice cold.

He heard the LAV squeal to a stop and prepared for another assault.

"Mathews, keep your head down. We're engaging the second LAV."

Hundreds of rounds blistered the BHR agents as they exited. A tick later, a voice broke over the BHR radio.

"Agent in Command Wolfe for Squad Six, report."

"This is Squad Leader Fletch. Six is negative. I need a medic, I'm gut-shot. Where did those shots come from?"

"Hold position, Fletch. Squad Four, breach that fucking dwelling!"

"Mathews," Lisa's panicked voice cracked over the radio. "We don't have a shot."

Mathews forced himself to his knees, his chest protesting his every movement. He locked eyes with Randy, flashed two fingers, then pointed at the door. Both men flinched as dozens of rounds blasted through heavy oak, spraying the interior with copper-jacketed death.

CHAPTER 59

OA, DAY ONE, CAMP LEJEUNE

Confusion quickly replaced Sergeant Bixby's shock as the government cell phones of every single Marine seated in Tinian Hall screeched to life. The message enraged him. Marine Corps Air Station Beaufort had fallen, with two hundred warfighters slaughtered. He understood they were next. The LAVs surrounding the hall were surely there to finish them.

Commanding Officer Slats, who'd been closely guarded by a pair of BHR agents, stared at his Marines. "Leathernecks," he shouted, his voice raspy with anger. "*Oorah!*"

Tinian Hall exploded. The BHR agents lining the walls proved wholly unprepared for the onslaught of four hundred Marines. Political affiliations vanished as the warfighters decimated their enemy. Without firing a shot, the lives of twenty-six BHR agents ended.

"Give me four companies, a hundred each," Bixby yelled. "If you have a weapon, you're on point. Find a window, go low, and wait for my order."

Realizing he'd usurped command, Bixby glanced to Slats. The CO gave a stiff nod, racked the slide of his 1911, and joined the ranks.

"The rest of you scour the supply room for chafing fuel, liquor—anything flammable. Move!"

Minutes later, Bixby stood with one hand on the door handle, a flaming Molotov cocktail clutched in the other. They were running out of time. The BHR agents huddled in their LAVs, unaware the Marines had seized control, would soon consider the lives of their comrades inside Tinian Hall moot and launch their attack.

"Now!" he yelled to the contingent of petrol-bomb-wielding Marines stationed at entryways throughout the building, and pushed through the door.

Covering fire erupted from Tinian Hall's windows, catching dozens of BHR agents flatfooted. Bixby saw the turret gunners tracking for targets. Unsure where the attack had originated, their return fire was delayed.

The first petrol bomb shattered against the turret of a LAV positioned to the west. The gunner's screams drew the attention of the turret gunner Bixby had targeted. He launched his bomb as his left leg was swept from under him. The pain revealed itself as he slammed to the ground. An enemy's bullet had removed his calf.

Despite the pain, he never lost sight of his target. The last thing he saw was his enemy swallowed by fire. Bixby died smiling.

***

In forty minutes, an outgunned group of Leathernecks raised the flag of the United States over Lejeune's main gate. Slats gazed at his remaining three hundred and sixty Marines. They were America's line in the sand. A line he intended to hold.

Chapter 60

OA, Day One,
Tremont

Billy turned onto West 11th and slammed the accelerator to the floor. His Citizen Soldier radio crackled with requests for backup, medical evacuations, reports of jammed or malfunctioning weapons, and scared soldiers begging for their mothers as they died. The broadcasts morphed into a jumble of voices telling the story of a country fighting back.

"This is Sergeant Billy Ash approaching the BHR squads at Lincoln Park. Don't fire on my vehicle. I'm dumping my soldiers at the front door. Clear a path."

"This is Agent in Command Wolfe. Stand down, soldier."

Ignoring Wolfe, Billy powered up the LAV's floodlight and focused it on Willis' home, providing Lisa, Max, and Watt a clear view of any threats lingering in the area. He pulled a sharp breath. Two agents had rushed onto the porch, barreling toward the front door.

***

Debris from the barrage hung in the air as the first BHR agent kicked through the remnants of the shattered entryway. He stepped right, allowing the trailing agent to enter. Both quickly dropped to a knee as Billy's floodlight suddenly illuminated the interior.

"Lisa Stinger, you're under arrest!" the first agent shouted.

Three loud bangs pulled their attention to the living room over their right shoulders. Randy broke cover and opened fire, lacing the agents across their chests.

***

"Lisa Stinger for Agent Wolfe."

Wolfe stared, disbelievingly, at his radio. "Where are my men?" he shouted.

"Stop asking stupid questions and listen to me. Tell your troops to stand down. End the bloodshed—"

"Shut your filthy mouth," Wolfe interrupted.

"I was hoping you'd say that. Church tower, you are a go."

The .338 Lapua round plowed through Wolfe's rear windshield, driving his head into the steering wheel. A split second before Lisa heard the rifle's report, the blaring horn from the agent's car served as a testament to the sniper's accuracy.

***

Billy maneuvered his vehicle between the Bureau of Harm Reduction's abandoned LAVs and backed it up to the porch stairs. Moving quickly, he punched the button to lower the hatch, radioed Mathews to evac, and began dragging the bodies of Thatcher and Rodriguez from the troop hold.

"Is that Thatcher?" Mathews asked as he hobbled past Billy, clutching his ribs.

"It is. Are you wounded?" Billy dipped his head toward Mathews' grip on his side.

"I'm good. Need a minute to regroup, but I'm still in this fight."

Billy spun, gripping his pistol as a hand came down on his shoulder. A broad smile creased his features as Randy wrapped him in a hug. They hadn't seen each other in nearly two years. It felt good!

"You're still ugly," Randy signed after releasing his friend.

"You're still big as a horse and smell like one too," Billy signed back. "Help with the bodies. Then, we pick up Lisa."

Randy held Thatcher's feet; Billy had his arms as they struggled down the ramp, fighting to keep their balance.

"Why didn't you just toss his ass out the back? That's the proper way to dispose of trash," Mathews yelled.

The first shot caught Billy in the neck, severing his spinal column, ending his life seconds later. Randy stared, confused. He couldn't hear the shot that killed Billy or the shot that ended his own life.

"No, no, *no*!" Mathews screamed, charging onto the loading ramp as a third round sliced through the air, slamming into the armor plating an inch above his head. He threw himself backward. His head met the steel floor and knocked him unconscious.

"Son of a bitch! Tower, where'd those shots come from?" Max hollered as he swung his rifle's scope, trying to locate the shooter's hide.

"No clue," Platt answered, his powerful scope sweeping the area. "Got him. Shooter is on a rooftop north of your position."

A shot rang out an instant later.

"Shooter is down. Area is secured."

***

Lisa sobbed into Randy's lifeless chest.

"I'm so sorry, my friend. I'm so very sorry. Please, God, don't let this happen. Please, no, God! Why?"

Max and Watt carried Billy into the troop hold, laying him gently on the floor. Max looked at Watt and nodded. They had to go.

"Lisa, I'm sorry. It's time."

Lisa sat on her heels as they lifted Randy from the ground, her pain so great it rooted her in place.

"The shooter's name was Aegir Elden," Bartle, one of Max's snipers, reported as he arrived at the LAV. "He's a Citizen Soldier and was working alone. Max, we didn't see him. He was set up behind the building's marquee."

Max had sent Bartle to confirm Aegir was dead and to secure any intel he was carrying.

"It's not your or Platt's fault. No one's blaming you. Keep your head in the game." Max spun a slow circle, addressing the group. "Let's load up. Armin's expecting us."

Lisa glared at Max. "Let Armin know we'll be late. We have a stop to make."

Max cocked his head. He was looking at Lisa questioningly when the perimeter device at the rear of the house detonated. The BHR was still on the hunt.

Chapter 61

OA, Day One,
Enlightenment Camp Alpha, Mojave Desert

"I say again, Enlightenment Camp Alpha calling EC Bravo, do you copy?" Sergeant Phelps had been frantically requesting reinforcements for thirty minutes to no avail. Every government entity within one hundred miles of EC Alpha had either not responded or refused to commit resources as they fought to crush a growing revolt. Now, EC Bravo, located three hundred and forty miles south, had gone dark.

Phelps raised the radio to his mouth to ready another plea when Corporal Spangler burst into the communications center, one of the camp's few remaining secured locations.

"Sergeant Phelps, I'm unable to report on casualties because the detainees have overrun the medical center." Spangler paused, meeting Phelps' anxious stare. "Sir, we've lost the receiving center. It's been annihilated. Ninety percent of our guards were either killed or wounded. Hundreds of detainees are dead, hundreds more have escaped. They've armed themselves with weapons scavenged from our dead."

Phelps' eyes closed tightly. A deflating breath escaped his lungs. "Leave. Escape if you can. I'll announce a full evacuation. Camp Alpha has fallen."

***

Dale Billson wheeled the BHR transport onto Interstate 40 East toward Route 95. By his estimation, they'd arrive at Enlightenment Camp Beta in six hours. He glanced at the side mirror and smiled. Three additional detainee-laden transports were trailing behind him. In their wake, hundreds of new arrivals streamed on foot from the gaping fissure they had created as they rammed their transport through the camp's south gate.

"I'm repentant about Lark," Margaux whispered in his ear. "I couldn't go back for her. Once she broke free of my grasp, she vanished into the chaos, literally swallowed by a sea of desperate humanity. When the guard towers unleashed their maelstrom, it became compulsory I seek the sanctuary of the transport."

Dale shook his head. "Your actions were neither malicious nor negligent. Lark's mental state had deteriorated rapidly. I feared her existence would end by her hand at any moment. I'm hoping she survives and receives the psychological attention she so desperately requires. If not, her outcome was inevitable."

"So brave of you. Your courage inspires me," Margaux paused, wanting to pivot to the task at hand while not appearing heartless. "Dale, you confirmed our plot with Spangler, correct? Additionally, we must address Doctor Malinger. I deem him untrustworthy, an impediment to our goal."

"Yes, my friend and taskmaster, I conferred with Spangler as the first detainees arrived. We will rendezvous outside Enlightenment Camp Beta, collect loyalists, and begin our trek to right this ship. We'll deal with the good doctor accordingly. Can you feel it? We begin rewriting history today!"

Margaux and Dale, distracted by their vision of taking the helm of a country they would redefine, failed to notice the commandeered Light Armored Vehicle speeding across the desert, tracking an intercept course to their caravan.

The resistance soldiers dispatched from their ad hoc base outside of the city of Parker and en route to Camp Alpha were heavily armed and operating under orders to engage government vehicles on sight. They followed these orders the instant Dale's transport fell into the range of their .50 caliber main gun.

Chapter 62

OA, Day One,
Cornelius, North Carolina

Callahan watched his men round up the last of the BHR agents who'd attacked his home.

"Lock them in the root cellar. If they're uncooperative, shoot them."

The BHR agents surrendered quicker than Callahan had ever witnessed a military force capitulate during his military career.

Callahan's team had dropped the first combatant entering his home the instant the agent identified himself. The man's arrogance and lack of discipline proved as deadly as the M4s awaiting him a step beyond the threshold. The kill box Callahan devised left the agent grossly exposed and caught unaware with little hope of survival. Three trailing agents met the same fate. The encounter finished within sixty seconds.

He'd felt a pang of worry when the second LAV arrived, but it quickly became apparent that those agents weren't interested in exiting their safe space to support their comrades, choosing instead to engage Callahan from the vehicle's turret. He'd have forfeited his freedom to witness the reaction of the agents when the turret gunner slid, nearly headless, back into the troop hold.

He coaxed them out by holding a flaming petrol bomb above the open turret hatch. The threat of death by fire provided ample motivation for the seven remaining BHR agents.

"Where to, boss?" MM asked, interrupting Callahan's mental recap of the swiftly won battle.

"Raleigh. We link up with the Leathernecks from Cherry Point, neutralize the Raleigh Citizen Soldiers' HQ, sweep the city's streets, take the fight to the BHR, and take back the capital."

"Oorah," MM growled through gritted teeth.

Callahan grinned. America's future rested in their calloused, blood-soaked hands. They would not fail her.

Chapter 63

OA, Day One,
CS Headquarters, Cleveland

Max pulled the LAV into the CS parking lot as BHR agents dragged a man by his bound feet toward a bus. A frenzied woman slapped and punched the soldiers as the man bounced off the pavement, struggling to remove the restraints binding his wrists. A guard rewarded her protest with a brutal gut punch, crumbling her to the pavement.

The man twisted as the soldiers dragged him past the woman's unmoving body.

"Shelly!" he screamed, his anguish rising above the chaos.

"Jesus," Max gasped as the CS grounds came into full view. Countless coach-style buses lined the perimeter waiting for hundreds of zip-cuffed citizens to be offloaded from dozens of LAVs, processed, and then shoved aboard.

"I didn't expect this. The IX Center must still be without power," Lisa muttered, her gaze sweeping from side to side. "Hit and run?"

"That'd be my choice. Mathews, Watt, hit and run?"

"Just set up a clear sightline, Max." Mathews was staring at the bodies of his friends, his response cold and detached. Max recognized what was happening. Mathews was preparing for battle.

Max twisted, searching for Watt's answer. He found the man seated on the floor, his BDUs spattered with blood, his eyes hard. He nodded his approval, stood, pulled his M4s charging handle, and moved into position at the rear hatch.

"Pratt, you're with me. Engage hostiles trying to flank us. Bartle, you're in the turret. Target drivers, buses, or both. Lisa, Mathews, Watt, I'm going to pull right and then back up. When the hatch lowers, you'll be facing a target-rich environment. Concentrate your fire on the soldiers at the rear of the LAVs. Bonus points for killing their drivers. If you don't have a clear shot, don't hover on the target. Move to the next one. Then, we double-time to the fallback. "

Max didn't wait for a reply. He stomped on the accelerator, yanked the steering wheel hard to the right, and set their plan in motion. Lisa stumbled against the LAV's sharp maneuvers as she rushed to join Mathews and Watt. The three of them took a knee and shouldered their weapons in unison.

"Weapons hot," Max yelled as they jerked to a stop and the hatch began its descent. "Fire at will!"

Bartle drew first blood, killing a driver at the front of the line. Then he worked methodically to disable the row of idling buses. Windshields splintered and engines were destroyed as shocked agents hesitated, confusion freezing them mid-step. Their indecision allowed detainees to break free and scramble for cover.

Gooseflesh raised the hairs on Max's neck as the combined battle cry from the cargo hold rose above the din.

Lisa's red dot bounced from target to target, hot brass rained to the floor, each empty shell signaling another kill. As their enemy's bewildered haze cleared, rounds pinged against the LAV's thick armor plating; they were running out of time.

"Go, go, go," Watt hollered when he noticed a LAV attempting to maneuver around a disabled bus.

The hatch began to rise, forcing the trio to continue firing from standing positions. Within seconds, it sealed and ended their assault.

"Talk to me, Bartle."

"Two LAVs attempting to give chase. Max, I don't believe what I'm seeing. People, including soldiers, are blocking their egress. Hundreds of them."

Lisa glanced at the men at her sides and nodded, a message crossing between them. They had just rained sparks onto a powder keg.

Chapter 64

OA, Day One, EEOB

Jack, eyes locked on Woods, bolted through an opening in the crowd created by the security details assigned to Stein's colleagues as they tried to restore order. The gray suits' fervor merely grew as the security details pulled individuals from the mass and zip-cuffed them.

"UW, on my six," he shouted. His words scarcely audible above the shrieking gray suits.

He leaped to the stage, unsure if his uncle heard him, and moved to intercept Woods and Cummings before they could escape with the President.

As he halved the distance to his target, the bottleneck's cause became apparent. Several bodies lay crumpled at the emergency exit's threshold, clogging the already tight space. Gray suits who'd attempted to navigate around their trampled colleagues found themselves hopelessly pinned against the doorframe. Secret Service agents pushed and pulled, trying to free them, but their efforts proved futile.

Woods cast a worried glance over her shoulder and locked eyes with Jack. She released her grip on Genus with a shove, sending the disorientated woman crashing into the mob and knocking Cummings to the floor.

Woods retreated to the rear of the stage, searching for a path to freedom but finding only escalating chaos. She focused on the podium where Stein fruitlessly continued his attempt to restore order to the auditorium. The large monitor serving as Stein's backdrop flashed scenes of the pandemonium outside the EEOB. America's streets resembled a battlefield in some far-off land as everyday citizens reclaimed their country. The images fueled the panic that had rooted deep into the souls of every gray-suited bureaucrat currently fighting to escape. Their empire was crumbling.

Jack read her body language. She was going to move on Stein.

"Not another step," he shouted, shouldering his rifle.

Woods' eyes widened as movement from behind the OA flag caught Jack's attention. Woods followed his stare. Her posture changed, relaxing as an old man shuffled into view.

Continuing his menacing approach, Jack screamed, "Both of you, on the ground!"

"Alois!" Woods shouted, stepping behind the man as his hand disappeared beneath his dusty suit jacket. The fluid and blindingly fast move caught Jack off guard. A split second earlier, he'd pitied the man for being used as Woods' human shield. Now, he stared into the muzzle of Alois' gun.

An instant before Alois fired, UW lunged toward Genus, who had her back to the threat. Willis hadn't noticed Jack until he fell to the stage. Momentum in control, he crashed into Genus, jolting her to the left as the bullet grazed her right shoulder.

Jack's shredded ear sent blood streaming into his mouth, igniting his fury. He fired from the floor. Alois' legs folded beneath him as he pulled the trigger a second time, sending the bullet careening toward the crowded exit where it found the base of Cummings' skull.

A three-round burst from UW's M4 ended Alois.

"Find Woods," Jack yelled, struggling to his feet and rushing toward the OA flag.

"Do you mean former Eastern Representative Woods?"

Jack, confused by Stein's calm demeanor, glanced to the podium. A wicked smile creased his features. Stein had Woods at gunpoint.

A hush fell over the auditorium as Jack stalked toward the bane of his existence. The woman who'd gleefully crushed his life. He pressed his M4's quick-release sling, letting his battle rifle free fall to the stage.

"End this now!" Jack growled as he unholstered his father's 1911. "Enough blood has been spilled. You've lost. Order your troops to stand down."

"You're a fool, *Mister* Stinger. An ignorant simpleton," Woods spat, her eyes blazing with defiance. "This," she continued, sweeping her hand to indicate the whole of government's bureaucracy. "There is no ending it, no standing down. It will swallow us all. Every corner of the globe is transforming as we speak. Therefore, Mister Stinger, you've merely prolonged the inevitable—"

Jack grabbed a fistful of Woods' hair, forcing her to face the monitor. Images scrolled alongside videos depicting a country in revolt.

"You caused this," he screamed, his face nearly touching hers. His blood sprayed on the side of her face. "You've killed thousands of people! Is that what you wanted?"

Woods smirked. "*You* caused this. The blood of One Americans everywhere is on your hands. I'm sorry, your *patriotic* hands."

His 1911's muzzle was pressed against Woods' head before she finished. Jack disengaged the safety, his finger taking up the trigger's pretravel. He visualized her head snapping to the side as the heavy .45 caliber round blasted through her temple. Jack screamed as he fought his rage. His desire to kill the woman sent tremors through his body.

Finally, he straightened and looked at Stein. "Lock this bitch up. Get her out of my sight. Death's too easy. She rots in prison."

Woods, a bead of sweat trickling down her cheek, glared at Jack and whispered, "Coward."

Woods' teeth shattered as Jack's fist slammed into her mouth, sending her unconscious body crashing to the floor.

CHAPTER 65

JANUARY 20TH, EEOB AUDITORIUM

"Your ear's going to look like you were brawling with Mike Tyson. All things considered, you're lucky."

"Thanks. Remember what I said: Woods gets no pain meds."

The medic smiled. "I remember, Jack. Not even baby aspirin, no matter how much she begs."

Jack found UW huddled with several military officers. They'd set up a table in front of the monitor, directing the revolt as it raged across the country. He marveled at how swiftly these men transitioned back into their roles as leaders and how rapidly the military had responded.

"How's it going?" Jack asked as he sat next to UW.

"Overall, better than expected. Word of the slaughter at Cherry Point spread quickly through our military and served as a battle cry. They've established several forward operating bases outside OA strongholds. As expected, the West Coast is a challenge. We've seen heavy fighting and casualties, but we've taken control of the skies."

"Any more news from Lisa?"

UW shook his head. The memory of what they'd sacrificed sliced through his soul. "They're holding the emergency broadcasting network. OA is scrambling to take it back, but Max's team has put up a solid firewall. It won't hold forever, but we won't need it forever. Only long enough to convince our nation to fight."

"Will we—" Jack stumbled, choked by emotion.

"We'll make it in time. I guarantee it."

Stein pushed through the side door, interrupting them. His grim expression an ominous sign of his conversation with Genus.

"It's Rosos. He's behind all of this shit. He's conspiring with Zhang."

UW pivoted and glared at Stein.

"Yes, Willis, that Zhang! We're dealing with the entire CCP. We've scrambled the Third and Seventh Fleets, but it'll take months to get them battle-ready. Our cyber teams are digging through our systems, trying to sever their links and bring our East Asia satellites back online, but OA is holding tight. They know what happens if we shake free. Willis, we picked one hell of a fight."

"They won't move on us. They'll wait us out, see if we destroy ourselves. They've never been interested in a hot war with the United States, but they were masters at chewing us up from the inside."

"They've got thousands of men here already. They're in a perfect position to launch on us," Stein shot back.

"But they didn't count on us fighting back. Genus tipped their hand during her address. China's objective was to be our saviors, have us welcome them with open arms. If they wanted a war, they would've attacked after Roberts and Eden were assassinated. Woods and Cummings wouldn't have offered any military resistance. But we hadn't been sufficiently worn down, weren't completely out of the fight." UW paused, thinking through their next moves. "Shut the borders down and shift some forces to our major ports. Bomb them if necessary. Just shut them down. *Now!*"

As Jack faded into the background, watching his uncle take control, he realized UW was in his element. He was where he belonged, where the country needed him: at the helm.

Understanding what was happening, Jack smiled. UW was entering the next phase, a phase that would separate them and send them to opposite corners of the country. He was at peace with it.

Chapter 66

Two Days Post OA, Conference Call

"Ah, Mister Rosos, I'm pleased you could join me. I trust you've witnessed the events unfolding in OA?"

"Zhang, don't be an ass. The entire world witnessed *your* failure."

"Blame, sir, is an animal best dissected in the future. Today, I'd like to know your plan for countering this revolt."

"This is *your* failure," Rosos shot back. "I told you we were not ready, but your arrogance blinded you. Your quest for the praise of your ruling class drove your actions, not reason. It is you who will devise a remedy."

"Mister Rosos, control of one's temper is a virtue unknown to you. It is a trait I've grown tired of—as I have you."

Rosos felt a chill roll down his spine as his office door swung open slowly.

"Remy," he barked to his assistant. "I was clear with you, I'm not to be disturbed."

Rosos gasped as Remy's head rolled to a stop at his feet.

"I take it your dear Remy isn't well. Please give Zi my regards. Good day, Mister Rosos."

A fist slamming against his office door interrupted Zhang's maniacal laughter. It was time to pay the cost of failure—a price Zhang would pay with his life.

Chapter 67

July 4th, Post OA, Outpost One

The morning dew soaked through Jack's BDUs as it had every morning since he arrived at Outpost One six months ago.

"It's your favorite day, Randy. Won't be the same without you." He paused, taking a sip of coffee. "Billy, I'm not sure how you felt about Independence Day, but I'm sure Randy will school you on an acceptable level of enthusiasm."

"Jack," Lisa called to him from their cabin. "UW's at the gate, he'll be here in a couple. Tell Randy I said hi."

"Well, boys, it's that time. Keep an eye on us. I'll bring UW up to visit. "

From atop the gently sloping hill overlooking the outpost, Jack could see UW's Humvee approaching from the east. The sight quickened his step.

A string of obscenities greeted him as he stepped onto his cabin's porch.

"Mathews, what the hell's wrong now?" he asked, raising his voice to be heard across the courtyard separating their cabins.

"I dropped the damn charcoal! Shit went everywhere. I just swept my cabin last week. Now it's a filthy, soot-covered mess."

"I don't care about the mess, but you best have enough charcoal for tonight. Max took a deer yesterday and we're planning on cooking the entire thing—every delicious morsel. For that to happen, we'll need every ounce of your fancy homemade charcoal."

UW's Humvee squealed to a stop between them and drowned out Mathews' angry mumbling. Jack, anxious to see his uncle, started to move from the porch when Lisa bolted through the cabin door, pushed him out of her way, and wrapped UW in a hug the instant his boots hit the ground.

"I've missed you too, Lisa."

Uncharacteristically emotional, Lisa simply tightened her hug and buried her face in UW's broad chest.

Jack held back, enjoying the scene. He allowed them their moment of normalcy, something they all longed for.

***

UW looked up from the gravesite, ending his prayer with a stiff nod and a sharp tug on his BUD's blouse.

"Burying them here was an excellent choice; it's always been one of my favorite places on the property."

"I agree. They can see the whole outpost from here and watch over us."

"Speaking of favorite places … You know, Ohio is secure. You can move back to the city."

"Nah. Being trapped in a city again isn't appealing. Plus, this is an important outpost. OA never found us, probably never will. We've launched dozens of successful operations from this place. Its location is perfect, which, I suspect, is why you bought it."

UW winked, a crooked grin creasing his leathery features.

"How are things going? The reports we've seen are encouraging, but I'd rather hear it from you."

UW's smile faded as his eyes darkened. "Other than a few hotspots, we've pushed them back to the Rockies. It's been a bloody, gut-wrenching process, but we're winning. There's talk of ceding California to them and constructing a wall if they agree to end hostilities. I'm not in favor of giving them a damn thing, but I understand the Joint Chiefs' reasoning. End it now, save some lives, and rebuild."

"If we give them anything, they'll declare victory, rally their base, and the entire thing starts over. I'm with you. Beat them into the ground."

They were quiet for a while, letting the sun warm their faces.

"How much longer, UW?"

"More years than I have left, Jack."

Jack breathed deeply. He'd already known the answer but found himself unprepared to hear the truth spoken.

"Jack? One favor. When we win this thing, guard this beautiful country. Guard her with a vigilance never seen before. Despite her flaws, she is the greatest country to have ever existed."

Jack slung his arm across his uncle's shoulders as they watched the sun explode in the eastern sky, a promise unspoken. His vigilance would be eternal.

The End

This marks the end of the Consent Of The Governed Trilogy. I'd like to thank you for reading my books. You can't know how much I appreciate you.

When I started the Consent Trilogy, I planned to inject the same level of humor as I had with my The Divided America Zombie Apocalypse Series. Although I brought some humor to this story, it took on a more serious tone that guided the story through its conclusion.

I hope you never forget what we have. America is indeed the greatest country to have ever existed. She is worth fighting for.

OTHER BOOKS FROM B.D. LUTZ

The Divided America Zombie Apocalypse Series
Divided We Fell
Of Patriots And Tyrants
A Dangerous Freedom
Eternal Vigilance

The Consent of The Governed Series
Silenced
Citizen Soldier

Reviews are invaluable to independent writers. Please consider leaving yours where you purchased this book.

Feel free to like me on Facebook at B.D. Lutz/Author Page. You'll be the first notified of specials and new releases. You can email me at: CLELUTZ11@gmail.com. I'd love to hear from you.

ABOUT THE AUTHOR

I was born in Cleveland, Ohio and now live in NEO (North East Ohio) with my wonderful wife (she told me to say that).

In my early adult life, I spent time as a Repo-Man for a rent-to-own furniture company and bill collector. Then I decided that was a tough way to earn a living and spent twenty-seven years working my way through sales management in corporate America. I've always wanted to write books, and I realized that we, you and me, have about fifteen minutes on the face of this planet and I needed to do one of the things I had always wanted to do. And, well, this is it.

If you're wondering, yes, I'm a conservative, I own guns, and I hate paying taxes.